FISH IN EXILE

VI KHI NAO

COFFEE HOUSE PRESS
Minneapolis
2016

Nao

Coffee House Press books are available to the trade through our primary distributor, Consortium Book Sales & Distribution, cbsd.com or (800) 283-3572. For personal orders, catalogs, or other information, write to info@coffeehousepress.org.

Coffee House Press is a nonprofit literary publishing house. Support from private foundations, corporate giving programs, government programs, and generous individuals helps make the publication of our books possible. We gratefully acknowledge their support in detail in the back of this book.

LIBRARY OF CONGRESS CATALOGING-IN-PUBLICATION DATA

Names: Nao, Vi Khi, 1979- author.

Title: Fish in exile / Vi Khi Nao.

Description: Minneapolis : Coffee House Press, 2016.

Identifiers: LCCN 2016007062 | ISBN 9781566894494

Classification: LCC PS3614.A63 F57 2016 | DDC 813/.6—dc23

LC record available at https://lccn.loc.gov/2016007062

ACKNOWLEDGMENTS

For Jeanne, who is kind and generous.

Excerpt on pages 58–59 is from "Si mi voz muriera en tierra" by Rafael Alberti, published in his collection *Marinero en tierra*, © 1924, El alba del alhelí, S.L. Reproduced with permission.

The drawing on page 168 is courtesy of the author.

PRINTED IN THE UNITED STATES OF AMERICA

23 22 21 20 19 18 17 16   1 2 3 4 5 6 7 8

FISH IN EXILE

CONTENTS

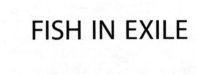

FISH IN EXILE

DEMETER BY THE SLANTED

ear of wheat bends over the earth calling, daughter
sinking into the heartbeats of foliage, land basks in
the abyss,   assault   in   the   abyss

"the face of Demeter dips her facade into the taut
stomach of dying snow" calls death insincere or a
perennial consideration of Hades's obsession with
Persephone, pomegranate arises   from   its loam

purplish mourning adds to the lips of distillation and
the seeds of the red gelatinous flesh that extend into
Lucifer, mouth   receives   the syntax of pain

gathering because the infinite arc of rape is in the
hands of the pollinators, Demeter cries into Zeus's
mouth to create her   infancy of   loss

ETHOS

I must think of myself first and get ahead. But the word *ahead* makes me sound like a sadist. A head. Someone's head, it seems to imply. Get a head. Outside, the wind is blowing leaves and dust across the meridian. The toilet hasn't completely dissolved the macerated toilet paper. At the bottom, a puff of cloud suspended. I stare at it hard for a long time, even long before the second flush. I keep staring at it as if it were my life: suspended between the ether of this world and sewage. I wish. Oh, I wish she had the courage to flush me down. The line between here and the alternate universe is just a flush away. After a while, the image becomes less depressing and more poignant, like going to the dollar theater with a tub of popcorn. It's just like that.

I remember being constipated and gazing down at the toilet bowl. She had fixed a blue disc to the inside edge of the bowl that made the toilet water blue like the sky. I watched as the adult meconium skyscrapers ascended the cloud. I like the idea of our shits going to heaven.

Once, I was caulking the bathroom floor because Catholic told me to. I always do what Catholic tells me to do. But I saw a cockroach running in and out of the cracks, so I timed it right. When the little fellow passed by, I caulked him to the edge of the wall. He tried hard to extend his head forward, to tear his legs from the viscid blanket of sealant. What if God were to treat me with the same kindness? What if he noticed that I keep running out of one hole and into another? What if he got annoyed with me! I hope he'd do me a favor and caulk me to the wall.

This morning, I stared at the refrigerator for an hour. I have other things to do. My wife tells me her carburetor stopped working and I need to fix or replace it. I told her I'd get to it. She doesn't ever listen. But I stared at the refrigerator for an hour because I listen to her. I actually listen to her. If I didn't, I wouldn't have stared at the refrigerator all morning wondering what to do. I stop by the junkyard's cemetery of car parts. I get derailed looking at the different types of rearview mirrors. They have all kinds. Rearview mirrors for a Toyota Corolla or a Nissan Sentra. I buy one for five dollars.

After the junkyard, I see Callisto waving at me from the bike shop. He waves, and then I wave. We are scheduled to see each other on Thursday. Today is Tuesday. I see him waving, and if I wave a bit more, and if waving a bit more leads to a decent conversation, it may mean that we have seen each other and Thursday's meeting may have to be cancelled. To be safe, I shouldn't wave anymore. I stop and he gives me a weird look. We're like syncopated swimmers. Seeming to fear that I have mistaken his wave for the breeze, he waves again with half his leg in the air. I climb into the car. I wave to him again. I can see some if not half of his leg in the air. It makes me realize how genuine his effort to see me is. The memory of his leg in the air grows painfully on the windshield. I have nothing planned for the rest of the week. I drive away without looking at him.

I carry a haversack with me now only to be in exile. I carry it with me even around the house. I begin to stare at the refrigerator. I stare at it hard for an hour. After that, not knowing what to do, I stuff items into my haversack. I stuff an organic orange into it. I stuff the haversack. The haversack stuffs my eyes. I wrap cubes of butter in wax paper and insert the cubes into the sack. I untwist the tie on a loaf of bread and take out three slices. I open the cabinet, grab the jar of peach jam, and insert it into the haversack. I stare at the wall. The refrigerator. The cabinets. Hours pass. The horizon disappears from view.

I have tasted the harshness of her lips. The angle of her chin, turned away from me in sleep. Love has a hard face. Hours pass. I am lured out of my exile to confront the curtain. I watch as the head of the cloud turns round and round. I have been staring long at the dank world before me. I have been staring at the chair for what seems like an hour now. The world is quiet. The chair is quiet. My mother is quiet, but she is not here.

My wife is quiet. She is not here, either. I am not sitting. Leaning. Nor standing on it. I am just here by the chair. Its four legs; my muscles rub against the front leg. It is quiet here next to the log. This morning, I looked at her face on the bed. The forest was our witness. I looked at her face. I have stared at her for so long. At the uncertain road ahead of us. She asked me to participate in the future. I replied: I'm in exile, can't you see? She didn't understand. We have gazed far into the distance before. On the balcony, she was sipping tea from the ocean, and I had my fingers wrapped around a Corona. Sometimes I paused to hear her breathe.

She was diaphanous. I could see through her. Her lungs exposed beneath a thin coat of rice paper. Could she see through me? We spoke every now and then about returning to the sea. Where the waves would weather us from the emptiness of the bovine. I sipped from the well of the Corona. The head of the clouds turned round and round.

I return to the bedroom and am startled to find her spread out on the comforter. Her closed eyelids are like two eggshells. I stare at my briefs.

I remember the earlier days. Now, before my wife, I am so small. I leave the threshold of the bedroom and walk into the kitchen. I pull open the drawer near the refrigerator and take out a pair of scissors. Walk along the wall of the house until I reach a path into the garden. Stare at the daisies pointing their yellow eyes at the sun. The roses, the tomatoes, the turnips, the clusters of sorrels, and the eggplants gather around the daisies. A floral séance. Walk up to the daisies and cut seven heads off a cluster. Lift the waistband of my briefs and put the heads of the daisies inside. I push the vagrant parts of the daisies deep inside my briefs so they're full and so even a leaf won't be mistaken for pubic hair. I return to the kitchen and insert the scissors back into the drawer. I go into the bedroom. My wife is still sprawled out on the comforter, hair spilling over the pillow like lacquer. Before I approach, she opens her eyes. Her eyes become wide. And then wider.

CATHOLIC: Come here, Ethos.

I walk slowly to the bed. Afraid. The daisies move inside my briefs like wilted paper. A quietly rasping eulogy. I can hear them talking.

Perhaps observing their own funerals. Walk slowly. The distance from door to bed is long.

I arrive, and she runs her right hand over my chest. The sound of her lingering on my oxford shirt syncopates with the frangible voice of the daisies. Before I know it, I am above her, longing. My head shortens the light illuminating her face. Her right hand continues to circle my chest. She strains her neck to reach for my face with hers. I feel the intensity of warmth, the responding fever of her kisses. I am rocking my body into her body. The violent friction of the pelvises.

After all, she is my wife. Her body against me, rubbing infinity into our spines. I lift her blouse above her head. She touches my shoulder, signaling me to turn over. We take turns sharing light.

Before her I see our babies roll over, turning into cold stones.

She lifts the waistband of my briefs and lowers it to my thighs. The daisies crawl out, falling onto the comforter like confetti.

My wife stares at my eyes, and then at my deflowered penis. She alternates this ping-pong gaze for five seconds before wiping the daisies swiftly from my penis and leaping off the bed. She sobs her way into the bathroom and closes the door. I lie on the bed and stare at the ceiling. I don't understand women or cameras. My thoughts are outnumbered by white diminutive dots. There are ants climbing up the slanted towers of my pubic hair to gaze into the milky horizon. I gently push them off my body with my palm. I know I should go to her. I crawl down onto the floor and hold myself in the fetal position.

The sobbing has receded into the wall. The only sound is the sound of my body on the floor. I stay there until the light passes through the house and returns to the bosom of the chthonic world. When darkness arrives through the windows, I lift my body up from the floor and walk toward the bathroom. It's wide open and unoccupied. My wife is gone. I am alone.

I go to the pantry and withdraw the dustpan from the shelf. I grab the broom from its place against the cans of chicken broth and walk back to the bedroom. I press the mouth of the dustpan to the floor and sweep the drooping daisies into it. They smell acidic. I take a handful and stuff it into my mouth. I chew it like tobacco.

I am on the phone with Callisto. My voice vibrates against my jugular flesh. I mumble something incoherent.

CALLISTO: I broke my tailbone having sex with Lidia. Do you think you can fix it?

No, I say.

CALLISTO: She threw me on the bed, but I landed on the bedpost. I think something's broken. Do you, by chance, have an MRI machine?

No, I say. You need a doctor. I can't help you.

CALLISTO: I have a fever and I can't ejaculate properly. Do you have any duct tape?

Yes, I say, I have duct tape. Do you want it?

CALLISTO: I'll be right over.

He leaves me hanging on the phone. I put down the receiver. I rummage through the house looking for duct tape. I remember it was in one of the kitchen drawers. But it is impossible to know now where I left it. In exile, duct tape is a luxury. I hear a knock at the front door. I think: How did he manage to get here so quickly with a broken tailbone?

I run to the DVD player and put in *La Notte*. The knocking continues. I fast-forward until I see the faces of Moreau and Mastroianni, then I sit down and stare at the screen. The knock comes again. Harder this time. I can't ignore it. So I open the door, expecting to face the face of a broken tailbone. It's Lidia.

> LIDIA: Callisto sent me over for the duct tape.

She is bulky, face-wise, and possesses talents not naked to the public eye. I am trying to grasp the meaning of the broken tailbone. Lidia is a little over five feet, petite, and has hair the color of fried octopus. Whenever I see her I want to chew on her hair. I can't imagine the impact this fried octopus has on that tall man, Callisto.

> ETHOS: What really happened to Callisto?
> LIDIA: He wants to duct tape his tailbone. He can't ejaculate properly, either. He's thinking of duct taping his scrotum too. I think it's a bad idea.

So he is telling the truth.

> ETHOS: I am watching *La Notte*, and I haven't a clue where the duct tape might be.
> LIDIA: Catholic might know.
> ETHOS: She isn't home.
> LIDIA: Where is she?
> ETHOS: She wasn't here earlier, but maybe she's back. Let me check.

I walk down the hallway. I see light piercing the bathroom door.

> ETHOS: Catholic?
> CATHOLIC: I'm in the bathroom.
> ETHOS: Lidia is here. She wants the duct tape.

CATHOLIC: We ran out. We used it all to send a package to
London for your mother.

I return to Lidia.

ETHOS: We shipped all of it to London.
LIDIA: Why would you ship duct tape to London?
ETHOS: London needs it.

To emphasize its gravity, I add, *badly.*

LIDIA: Callisto will be disappointed.
ETHOS: Why did your boyfriend sleep with my wife?
LIDIA: Apparently that's something some neighbors do.
ETHOS: We're not such neighbors, are we?
LIDIA: You never made the move.
ETHOS: It didn't occur to me.
LIDIA: You mean it doesn't appeal to you.
ETHOS: It does appeal to me, but it didn't occur to me.
LIDIA: But *appeal* and *occur* in this context are synonymous.
ETHOS: What context?
LIDIA: No context at all, apparently.
ETHOS: I like flowers on certain things. My wife doesn't like
flowers on anything.
LIDIA: I like flowers too. Callisto hardly gets me any. A
bouquet—small, very small—would be nice.
ETHOS: Would you like some daisies?
LIDIA: No.

I close the door on her face and face the wall. After about five minutes, I return to the evidence Michelangelo Antonioni left in the living
room. He is spilling all over the sofa, laminating it with a thin coat of
film. I stand in a pool of black-and-white images.
The phone rings.

CALLISTO: Has Catholic told you that she doesn't love you
anymore?

ETHOS: Not yet, but she will.

I think it's a decent response for someone who is unable to duct tape his scrotum. I do not like the way my wife smells when she's tearing me apart. I sit in a corner chewing the elbow of a baguette. I sit far from the sofa, nibbling on the crumpled elbow of the baguette, inside a pool of black-and-white images.

Catholic comes into the living room. I pull the haversack closer.

CATHOLIC: Go away.

I lower my head and she leaves the room. I tear the flesh of the baguette into pieces and jam it into my mouth. I take the butter from the haversack and peel the wax paper off. The outside world is knocking at my gate.

This is my body cheating death. This is my body creating life.

It is chilly here when I return from the sea. The spiders are out and so are the mosquitoes. Everything is blue like heaven. I tug the haversack closer to my body. I must now face the door. I stare at it, hard and cold. And then I release it. I release the grip of my eyes on it. The door softens. I am driven by the impulse of phlegm. I am tired and feel that closing my eyes is death. I won't shut my eyes. I woke up this morning from a strange dream. I have walked across the room in hopes of crossing out our life.

I am sitting by the window where the sun can receive me. This is where my darkness, in broad daylight, doubles. Here is my frame, solid and complex, flesh all alike, and there is my shadow, next to the microwave. I sit in exile where Catholic and I used to watch the sun lower his toga. I ask, is it better to be in exile at home or at home in exile? I labor over my fruit. I labor over my knowledge of my life and my marriage.

Over onion, garlic, sugar, and salt, my dear wife joins me. Over the haversack, I reveal the contents of my sparse, indigent thoughts to my wife. She turns away. Her face, her back, the turn of a century, the parting of one resilient cloud. Catholic turns, and we are away from each other. She is away from me, rather. Turning is toxic. As toxic as light pollution. When she turns her shoulder away from me, how her skin radiates then. Something in me dies this way every day. Her shoulder. When she turns and I'm able to take a closer look at her ear, her earrings come to me, dangling like branches on the tree of her ears. They are glittering limbs, suspended between her earlobes and shoulders. When Catholic turns her shoulder from me, something in me dies.

I watch as she pulls herself up. I see her heels lifting, removing stacks of thread from her footing. Each step is a swallow. A vacuum. I swallow the vacuumed space. Each step strikes me higher and higher in the stairwell of my loneliness. But this is not loneliness. Not the wall. Not the ending in the middle. She lifts her heels, and I jolt up and grab the haversack and tuck it close to my violent, dead heart. The garlic. The salt. The grapefruit. Her heels. My eyes chase after her heels. And when my eyes stop, so do her heels. I tap lightly on the shoulder that has turned away from me.

ETHOS: Catholic?

CATHOLIC: Ethos?

ETHOS: Where are you going?

CATHOLIC: I am going nowhere.

ETHOS: Are you sure?

CATHOLIC: Certainly.

ETHOS: Can I come with you?

CATHOLIC: No.

ETHOS: Why not? Why can't I join you?

CATHOLIC: I want to think of ways I can love you properly. Right now you're getting in the way of that contemplation.

ETHOS: Don't you think it would be good for me to be a part of this conversation?

CATHOLIC: You can't be involved, Ethos. You can't be involved in my happiness.

ETHOS: Don't you think this is wrong?

CATHOLIC: No.

ETHOS: I'm confused.

CATHOLIC: We are not two halves. We are not some bifurcated thing. Happiness is not a fluid. It doesn't contaminate the body of melancholy. It separates the chaff from the wheat. Think of it this way, love, you are solitude. Our marriage works because I've deserted you completely. Let me be and I'll love you properly. I assure you.

I watch her heels lift emptiness from the ground. Those footsteps. My longing. The heat of the home condenses. My thoughts expand. The contractual obligation of physicality in the face of ennui. Her shoulders come to me again. And again. I am alone again. To face the stairs. To face the falling body of the curtain, the blank wall, the canisters, the blender, the toilet paper, the beater, the garlic peeler. My wife has spoken about solitude. Has woken me up from the despair of my body. The despair of a life. This separation between married individuals. This disconnected and obscure and elliptical space between husband and wife. Am I now finally alone because she has a strong compass about our solitude? She is convinced of our separate paths in a united realm. What is solitude if not two parts (or more) emerging as one? Is this what she means? I don't understand.

I fall asleep in the chair. When my body wakes from its perennial flight, I walk my body into the bedroom. The world is moving slowly. Light shifts, lifting the four corners of the room into an origami box. As light moves around the sculptured paper, darkness begins to enclose me. Darkness falls on my chest and an involuntary impulse pushes the frame of my body toward the pillows, where a fetus or two may have crawled out to make room for my head. My head falls into the deflated pillow. My hands tucked between my thighs. I dream the earth is populated with blueberries. During REM, my body sprawls out involuntarily; my left hand overlaps Catholic's torso. The contact stirs me awake. My eyelids flutter open.

ETHOS: You were in my dream.
CATHOLIC: Ethos?
ETHOS: Where are you going?
CATHOLIC: I'm going nowhere.
ETHOS: Are you sure?
CATHOLIC: Certainly.
ETHOS: I dreamt that your placenta was packed with blueberries.
CATHOLIC: You mean my pancake?
ETHOS: No, your placenta.
CATHOLIC: Don't be foolish. Go back to sleep.

Catholic's eyes roll back into her head. Her head rolls back onto the pillow. Moonlight walks naked through the bedroom window, and I'm tortured with nostalgia. I turn my head to her profile. She lies on her back like a white mausoleum. She is white as stone. I am rigid. I turn my head to try to threaten my rigidity into movement, but my head falls into the abyss of the pillow. I dream that I kiss my wife's forehead before wrapping her body in a blanket of snow. I am naked, dehydrated, and cold. Afterwards, I try all day to unwrap her. Though I spend all day removing snow from her body, she is eternally covered with frozen water + atmosphere + vapor + ice crystals. I drift in and out of consciousness. I am awake again.

Catholic, lying next to me, is still a breathing stone. I try to breathe slowly and carefully, as I imagine a stone would, but my breath comes out of my nasal chimneys rustling like paper. The sound carries the neonatal memory of my firstborn, Abby, who would shift unpredictably from one place to another, her diaper rustling beneath her hyacinth dress. If she were here, she'd spread her fingers out on my stubbly cheeks. She'd scoop out spoonfuls of dreams from my head and insert them into the pillowcase. When finished with that, she would holler into the pillowcase and ask the dreams to come out and play. Awake and alert, I lift my body from the bed.

Hunger moves me into being. Nude, I walk away from the bedroom, and my body drifts toward the kitchen. The lids on the mason jars seem to contain not pickled onions or quail, but children's breath. Moonlight spills onto the pinewood table. I want to whisk the nocturnal yolk into my mouth. I remember kneeling here before my wife as her face receded in the darkness and her belly advanced. With my ears pressed to her belly, I listened for Abby and Colin, adrift in the embryonic moon and pulsating like a song. The wind twirls the curtain from the far window. I walk toward the drawer near the refrigerator. I grip the drawer and pull it toward me. I lift a spoon from the face of another spoon and shove the drawer until it cannot be shoved further. Then I turn my body to the moon. Before the moon, I stop.

I stop at two a.m.   At three a.m.   At four a.m.   I stop.

I stop. My breath is white. I dip the spoon into the insoluble surface of the moon. I shovel light urgently into my mouth. I try very hard. I try so hard my face turns white. Light spills between the cracks of my teeth. Craters stick to my premolars. I eat part of the moon in the kitchen like onion soup. Its liquid spills onto the china cabinet. The corner of the chair and counter. The edge of the cutting board. The pine table. A large pool of moon soup migrates onto the floor. The moon descends my Adam's apple and passes through my esophagus. When it falls past my rib cage, my organs—heart, lungs, gallbladder, liver, intestines large and small—glow in the dark.

I stand there eating quickly, trying to stuff Colin back into my mouth. The fetus. My wife's placenta. The spoon dips in and out of me, shoveling light and shadow into my mouth before the moon withdraws her onion soup back to the cosmos. When I am done, when the sun is about to poke its diurnal head through the clouds, and when there is no more moon to eat, I turn my heels to bed. I pass through the dark tunnel of the hallway and find my wife sprawled out on the bed like an island. She is naked, and I am nude.

I walk up to my briefs and grapple with them before donning them. I insert my body between the bedsheets and stare at the darkness, at the long interludes of empty hours. I try hard not to wake my wife or activate the sweat glands of her calves. Next to me, she is still, a breathing, dreaming stone. The darkness tries to latch its hinges to the morning hours, but dusk is a door that cannot be opened on command. I have a lot of time to contemplate the gesture of blankness and to complete it if it hasn't been fulfilled.

I reshift my body, trying to mold it into the bed. In the midst of shifting my body, my left hand swings involuntarily to the side of the bed, and the tips of my fingers brush against a tough material. I hold the fragile thing with my index and middle fingers like the wing of a blindly caught butterfly. A distilled, static image of a rope replays itself from the projecting slides of my consciousness in the theater of my head. I had wanted to be closer to the chandelier.

Memory, having revealed the identity of the obscure object, also reveals my hand's motive from yesterday's activities. Tips of the fingers grope for the rope. The edge of the rope's synthetic fibers etch an electrical road through the sandy, cloistering sadness of my membrane. Yes, this is where I had been, and this is where I am now. I grope the rope further into its history on the floor below the bed frame. A fragile thing, so open and so light, strokes tenderness and vulnerability into my fingers. Beating freely and weakly in the moist atmosphere of light and dark, a hyacinth. And soon, like a child that blooms into a hand, I fall asleep.

In the morning it rains. The drums of the rain shout into the ground, opening the curtain of November's wound. After a while, sex doesn't make sense. There are certain things about women I have learned over the years: they keep things concealed. Tupperware shopping is very important. I watch the rain fall while I shovel Cheerios from a porcelain bowl into my mouth. I woke up this morning from a strange dream. I dreamt of suitcases as funeral homes for children. I read somewhere that Einstein didn't think energy could evaporate.

My wife disappears around the corner, preparing for work. I place the Cheerios bowl in the kitchen sink. When I could fumble through her body in search of lost keys, love seemed real. There is nothing here anymore. I am giving my wife time to process bliss. So she can break us apart—we, the mechanical and chemical operations of happiness.

I stare vacantly at the windowsill. My hands flank my torso like arms of machines. The refrigerator notices me, so I open it and take out the eggs. I twist the cap off the extra-virgin olive oil and drizzle it into a frying pan. I crack three eggs in a porcelain bowl and whip them into a liquid the color and consistency of urine. I pour it into the pan as soon as the pan becomes hot. I salt and pepper for taste. At this point I see no reason to find work. I have seen enough of the indentured seasons. I have seen enough of death. I am, after all, in exile. At first I thought it was an existential asylum. Of my freedom and my fatherhood, taken from me unjustly. I feel displaced. I would argue that tragedy deported me here. Take me away from me. Take me away from my homeland. I'm a refugee inside my own home. I have abandoned my job, my vocation, my education, my subordinate employees, and adopted a lifestyle that is nearly uninhabitable.

Catholic, after rummaging in the bathroom drawer, reenters the kitchen. She has donned a red silk blouse tucked under an indigo linen knee-length skirt that sways between her black Audrey Hepburn kitten heels.

ETHOS: You are my wife.
CATHOLIC: Yes.
ETHOS: Where are you going?
CATHOLIC: I'm going to work.
ETHOS: Are you sure?
CATHOLIC: Yes.
ETHOS: What will I do?
CATHOLIC: I don't know.

I open the refrigerator and take three leaves of lettuce from a translucent container. I untwist the tie from the plastic covering the bread and withdraw two pieces. With a spatula, I forklift the scrambled eggs onto the bread. I am useful. I wrap the sandwich in tinfoil and put it in a paper sack for my wife. I am useful.

ETHOS: I'll get depressed.
CATHOLIC: You certainly will.
ETHOS: What will I do?
CATHOLIC: Be obsolete.
ETHOS: No, that's impossible. It's not a choice.
CATHOLIC: There are many fish in the sea. There are also many choices. I have to go!

I push the paper sack into her body, and she walks out the door. Her heels click as she descends into the street. Alone, I turn to face the wall. I stare at the daedal patterns on the wallpaper. I can smell the scent of egg yolk and of something arriving and departing. I want to write the world a letter.

Dear Ithaca,
In the morning, your beautiful left leg came to me
anatomically.

Ethos

Instead, I walk eight miles to the sea. To the cemetery. When I walk I can feel eternity in my throat. A barrel of sky in my throat, ready to cough its way onto the street. I walk with my haversack strapped to my chest like a hollowed-out defibrillator. Two cypress trees greet me on the way to the sea. Two cypress trees side by side, two feet apart. It must be cruel to be so close to another cypress and only linger, but not touch.

Light moves, shifts, stirs between clouds. The air is so still, and the grass, awake, lies dormant on the surface of the earth. Winter is approaching. I am afraid of her. Last year, October bowed her head low, afraid to look up, to gaze at anyone, passing through like a baby stroller. Winter held her white coat out like a rifle, ready to blow anyone's head off at any moment.

When my body approaches the undulating salt, the waves are breaking the back of the sea. They come crashing into the living room of sand. I stand there and think about the waves and the slanting nature of light, and God's hands torn out of his pockets as he folds my life, like a letter, into an envelope and inserts it into the mailbox of the sea.

A mailbox, after all, is where letters go to die. My life soaked in salt and seaweed before it's delivered to me on the living room of sand. My life flutters as it tries to crawl toward the salt water. I stand before God for hours while the sea roams. Salt-fermented clusters of air chase the outer rims of waves. Sun. Gun. Gone. Where is winter now when I need her to fire and split a bullet of light into two? I walk along the shoreline. Along the shoreline, there are hundreds, perhaps thousands, of desiccated jellyfish.

I once watched a dozen jellyfish carry their cloud-shaped tentacles across a home made of fluorescent twilight. These jellyfish, expired, do not look like clouds carrying thunderstorms on their backs, but wilted, sepulchral embryos. I dig into the haversack for a wrapper. I bend down and collect a pair of aquatic coelenterates and toss them into the haversack. I tear apart a piece of bread and take it into my mouth. Time elapses. I stand up and gaze onward. It's inevitable, then: my children must return home. I will take their aquatic, nomadic abode into our home. The wind breaks me open into the darkness. The sea blurs, and my thoughts blur with it. Night falls; light stands behind my body like a sentry. I make the eight-mile walk back home. How long have I been away? Perhaps my wife will be waiting for me with a plate of fried calamari.

Lidia is at the doorstep with a letter in her hand. I pass her to open the screen door.

ETHOS: Have you seen my wife?

LIDIA: No.

ETHOS: I'm sorry we couldn't make it to dinner the other—

LIDIA: It's alright. I'm sorry we forced you to come. Callisto can be brutal when he's feeling sensitive. Will you give this letter to your wife? From Callisto.

ETHOS: Of course.

LIDIA: Thank you.

I toss the letter into the haversack.

ETHOS: How's his tailbone?

LIDIA: Not good. He's in the hospital. In a lot of pain. I have to go.

ETHOS: Please come by again. Catholic and I will be sewing buttons onto shirts for Dogfish and Pistachio.

I watch Lidia descend the steps, then I enter the living room. The house is dark, somber, and cold. I turn on the living room lights and walk toward the kitchen. My empty stomach in an empty house. I open the refrigerator door. I glance past the kitchen faucet and gaze into the lighter stage of twilight. Highway and faucet. Water is dripping from somewhere. Half flushing, half drowsy, I close the refrigerator door and walk to the pantry and lift one can of anchovies from another and walk back to the sink. Dig into a drawer and take out a can opener. Press the lip of the can opener to the top of the can and roll its wheels. After two revolutions, I lift the lid with a butter knife, remove the haversack from my chest, and take out Callisto's letter to my wife.

His unscientific scribbling addresses Catholic from the midsection of the envelope. With Callisto in the hospital, my wife's clitoral stem should be safe and photosynthetically inactive. Where is my wife on a Friday evening? I take out the bread and set it on the counter. I stand like a fixture in the dark kitchen, chewing on bread dipped in anchovies. Fried calamari on a plate, I pretend. Sprinkled with parsley and marinara. Sometimes when I chew as slowly as I chew, I can't tell if the salt is tears or anchovy oil.

In old trucks, carburetors are finicky: sensitive to particles, to climate, to air, to residue, and to tinkering. Gasoline congeals in the carburetor's orifices, plugging the venturis with a gelatinous film. I lift up the hood of the 1987 Toyota. I disassemble the parts—Phillips screws, fuel needle, throttle shaft and plate, jet, slider, spring, carburetor body—and remove and discard the intake hose, which is like a vestigial organ. After five cans of choke and carb cleaner (B-12 Chemtool) on these parts and silicone spray on the choke rod, I put everything back together again, the parts shifting in and out of my vision. I try to remember their roles in the composition. I turn the engine on and the 4Runner idles smoothly. It's like clearing out the coagulated ink inside the sac of a squid. I walk to the side of the house and twist the nozzle of the hose. Water rushes into my hands, and I lather them with soap.

The mechanical squid is relentless in its buildup of carbon, muck, and rust as it prevents itself from having access to power. To clean the carburetor is a daunting task, and I don't know why I have waited this long to get the engine running when things need to be done. But the journey to the sea is irresistible. Without the sea, my wife and I do not have a home.

Light catches on Catholic's caliginous, misty hair as she pulls into the driveway. Her hair has grown past her shoulders and faded since last winter. Is it light or is it gray? She only turned thirty-three a few weeks ago. She walks up to me, radiating. Her hands are occupied with plastic bags. The translucent plastic gives me access to its contents: spools of thread, folded fabric, zippers, and buttons.

> ETHOS: Catholic?
> CATHOLIC: Yes.
> ETHOS: You came home very late last night.
> CATHOLIC: Did I? How unfortunate.
> ETHOS: Yes. Very late.

Light tosses in the air and seems to land solely on her face. She looks like olive oil spilled on a copper pan. She radiates, and I am afraid. The sun releases its glare; I squint.

> ETHOS: Why so late?
> CATHOLIC: Visiting a patient.
> ETHOS: How is he functioning?
> CATHOLIC: With massive doses of Vicodin.
> ETHOS: Are you in love with him?

Catholic turns her face to Lidia and Callisto's backyard. Their November garden, held up by wire frames, is an elongated chicken coop of wilted eggplants, hairy green onions, drooping sorrels, inelastic cucumbers, flaccid romaine lettuce, mulched rhubarb stalks, and putrescent tomatoes.

> ETHOS: Are you in love with him?

Her eyes lift to the sky, then drop to their purple siding.

> ETHOS: Are you in love with him?
> CATHOLIC: No.

I watch as she walks up the steps, shifts the materials to the left side of her body, pulls the screen door open with her unengaged hand, and slides her body into the house. I turn the nozzle off, wipe my aqueous hands on the thighs of my blue jeans. I walk to the truck and climb in, then I drive ten minutes to the hardware store. I pull into the parking lot. With the haversack thrown over my shoulder, I enter the store. I take out a blueprint and lay it flat on the counter.

ETHOS: Can you get me these materials?
CLERK: How soon do you need them?
ETHOS: Immediately.
CLERK: Let's see.

The clerk disappears into the back of the warehouse. The hardware store smells like sawdust and alloys. The clerk returns.

CLERK: We have everything but the Plexiglas. We don't carry
    it in that size. If you walk up to Sella Windows around the
    corner, they can help you out.
ETHOS: Thank you.
CLERK: Give us fifteen minutes to get everything together.

Outside, God is dragging his evening gown of masculinity across the sky. The sky is a relentless thing: constantly hovering, unforgiving, ready to substitute darkness for light. I walk down the street. At the end of the street is the Memory Athenaeum. It pierces the earth like a knife in a knife block. Darkness is contagious. The trees collect darkness beneath their wide armpits. Everywhere, everyone is collecting darkness. The woman who sits in her locked car, alone, the engine off, collects darkness on her shoulder, her hair, the tops of her nose and eyes. The clerk who twists the shutters of his windows closed. The little children dashing across cobblestones collect darkness in their mouths. When they uncup their hands after hollering the names of their comrades, darkness spills out. I walk to Sella Windows. The way I move and the way the earth is not moving as quickly gives me the impression that God is quietly spreading the thighs of two buildings yonder. I stop in the street and take the wallet from my jeans pocket. I open it to let darkness in and out. I want to know if I have enough cash for the Plexiglas or if I will need to charge it. It is ridiculous; I can't see the faces of the presidents clearly. I shut the wallet and enter the building.

CLERK: We're about to close.
ETHOS: I'm sorry.

Immediately after entering the store, I begin to exit it.

CLERK: Can I help you with something?
ETHOS: Oh. Yes.
CLERK: What is it, then?

The clerk's eyebrows lift toward the ceiling, shifting the frame of the monocle.

ETHOS: I want to order several dozen sheets of glass.
CLERK: What kind would you like?
ETHOS: What do you have?
CLERK: Well, depends on what you want to use it for. We have Grade A safety glass. It breaks like a heart: into millions of pieces as opposed to large slivers or chunks. We have laminated, polycarbonate, fiberglass, nonreflective glass for photo frames, annealed, mirrored, figure rolled, and—
ETHOS: I'll take Grade A.
CLERK: Are you building a window for a bank? It's—
ETHOS: Bulletproof.
CLERK: Right.
ETHOS: Which is the easiest to cut?
CLERK: Laminated. It's fairly nonthreatening.
ETHOS: I'll stick with that, then. Thirty-nine sheets, fifty inches by twenty. And two glass cutters, please.
CLERK: They'll be here in five to seven business days. You can pay when you pick up.

ETHOS: They can't come any sooner?

CLERK: Afraid not.

I navigate back to the hardware store. The exterior surface of the store is black, as if it has been hiding in a sackcloth. A man in beige overalls helps me lift the items from his warehouse into the truck: thirty tubes of silicone packed into a large grocery bag; three tubes of blue tape; twenty-five sheets of fiberboard, nine feet by four feet by half an inch; and three boxes of 100 common nails, each two inches long.[1]

---

1. At home, I stand before the refrigerator. The light pours out onto the darkness of the kitchen. The calcium I consumed earlier descends to lower grounds. My stomach aches. How the stomach explodes from the yogurt of yesterday's dream: a white cloud of calcium on the alimentary bowl of the stomach.

In the morning, I open the refrigerator and walk the frozen plate of my memory to the microwave. Submerge the memory in radiation to nuke the polarized molecules of my thoughts. I have come to an abrupt understanding of certain things: no mainland or minnows. Earlier, I spoke to Catholic about moving, moving our bodies into the mainland. But Catholic is unyielding. "We will stay," she said firmly and simply.

The unscholarly school of minnows that pushes the large shopping cart of the whale around the Walmart of the sea does not know that there is no aisle seven for fish sticks or tailgating. "We will stay" haunts me now. Perhaps I need to change the format of my love for her. Or the font. She simply has to be Garamond. Because I am Garamond. Yet no matter how I format it, it won't give. I stare at the microwave a very long time without opening its door. I sit down on the pinewood table, tear a sheet of paper from a notebook, and write a letter to the world with a black calligraphy pen:

Dear Moscow,
My mind is dizzied by the sound of infants. By the window &
its flat face. I roll myself into the barrow to block out the world
and all of its dizzy light & night. In bed, the dream sails me
into seven levels of consciousness. In the first level, I am dead.
In this state, I can feel the face of reluctance pressing on my
chest. I feel winter exchanging her rope for despair. For who
can tell the rhythms of day from night. My soul is a cul-de-sac.

Hormones, ingrown toenails. Growing in centimeters at a time. But I can feel it. Exchanging vows with each other about eternity. The hormones. The toenails. And then in the second level, my blood flows backward. Flows back out into the sea. I am an empty sack of flesh & weed. Fluttering in the four winds of my consciousness. I am blown from the west & then to the east, but never north nor south. In this level, I am yellow like the fever. No longer red like blood. In the third, my consciousness goes out into the field to collect my bones. My bones, like paint thinner, shrink overnight. Desiccated calcium. Painted inside the dome of my thoughts. Sometimes I can't tell if my bones are my bones. Or if Caravaggio has blown into my bloodstream & parked his paintings there. In the fourth, I can see near & far. I can distinguish the dark from the light. For instance, in the fifth, it's euphoria. It's located between the three lenses of consciousness. The first lens: indecision. The second: humility. The third: acceptance. None of these lenses speak to me. In the sixth level, I regain some formality. I am eating breakfast by the sea. My fingers make holes in the fabric of my lungs. Trying to light air. Ignite desire. Skin is breaking through the heavenly realm of my emotions. I can feel my breath. In the seventh, I am inside someone else's terminal illness.

Ethos

After the letter, I stare at the blank wall, the habitual state of my existence. Awhile later, while walking toward the pantry for some sun-flower seeds, I remember the Hot Pockets. Now, cold.

Catholic is having her tubes tied. The fight for it (for the tubes to have proper airflow, for an uninterrupted escape through the tunnels) has been very lengthy, and Catholic won in the end. She's closing her borders to traffic coming from North America, specifically, Canada and Mexico. The parliament, my wife, made an appointment with the gynecologist. They both acknowledged my testicular vote and excused me from their oval office. They made an executive choice that brings me to this morning. This morning, I'm driving her to the hospital. She wears a white blouse that smells like honeysuckle. On the way to the hospital, I pull up to a bookstore.

> CATHOLIC: You can delay the inevitable, but you can't stop it.
> ETHOS: I know.
> CATHOLIC: Will you be long?
> ETHOS: No. Would you like to come in with me?
> CATHOLIC: I'll wait out here. Please be quick, Ethos. I haven't
>   eaten anything, and I do feel short of patience.

Surreptitiously, I maintain a parliament of my own. I may have the support of the entire continent of Asia. While my wife is under an operating table sealing and severing all entry points, I bustle around the city. I open my passageways, my own silk road into my wife's body and, perhaps, heart. I walk around the city like a decapitated chicken, filling out form after form. The USCIS Form I-600A in particular. I write a check for the filing fee of $720. I stop by the post office and mail everything to this address:

USCIS
P.O. Box 660088
Dallas, TX 75266

Time is still on my side. Hours after the operation begins, my wife still hasn't been wheeled out of the bed in her floral hospital gown. As hard as I try to alter my perception of hospitals, they always exude the odor of an insane asylum and Windex. I walk my body back and forth across the hospital floor. My tennis shoes screech in the waiting room. I feel more at home as a designated driver for an inebriated wife than for a wife partaking in tubal ligation. Hungry, I dig inside my haversack. There is butter and bread at the bottom, and a pair of jellyfish that look more and more like fallopian tubes. *Les Fleurs du Mal* leans against the side of the haversack and brings my attention to Callisto. I stopped at the bookstore to grab a copy of this luminary Baudelaire for him and had forgotten it. I walk up to the registration desk and ask for his room number. I take the elevator to the right wing of the hospital, E7, to room 220. Book in hand.

His room is a transparent box. His tailbone is hidden in the white sheets of the hospital bed. At the sound of my footfall, he turns his puffed cheek to my entry. His eyes, soporific and hazy, shift from my face to the replay of the French Open final between Nadal and Federer. The Mallorcan is leading the first and second sets. After Nadal hits a winner, Federer prepares to serve.

CALLISTO: Please do not stare at me as if I were *Les Fleurs du Mal*.
ETHOS: Okay. I'm sorry.

I pull a chair up to his bed.

CALLISTO: Do you mind getting me some water?

He points to the sink in the adjacent partition. I walk to it and fill the cup and hand it to him.

ETHOS: He doesn't ever sweat, does he?
CALLISTO: Look at his hair. I want that hair.
ETHOS: It makes him look so effeminate.
CALLISTO: He's a perfect symbol of beauty. Just look at his face.
ETHOS: His face and his backhand are so weak and destroyed and—
CALLISTO: Eye on the immaculate forehand, man.

Callisto pushes the button on the remote control pinned to the table on wheels and the tube shuts off.

CALLISTO: I want. I want. I want. I want.

I hand him his gift from my hand, the Baudelaire book. Thick as a pineapple core. He holds it and cracks it open.

CALLISTO: Merci, man. *Là, tout n'est qu'ordre et beauté, / Luxe, calme et volupté.*
ETHOS: *Car j'ai, pour fasciner ces dociles amants, / De purs miroirs qui font toutes choses plus belles: / Mes yeux, mes larges yeux aux clartés éternelles!*
CALLISTO: The French preposition *du* means "fuck" in another language. I want that—
ETHOS: In Vietnamese.
CALLISTO: How did you know?
ETHOS: My father was in the wa—
CALLISTO: Right. Đụ má mày. Đụ ba mày. Đụ đụ đụ đụ.
ETHOS: Hmm . . . *du đủ* is a word for papaya.
CALLISTO: *Les fleurs du mal* roughly means "flowers fuck evil."
    Lucifer likes how perennial words reside on the ground of his heart.

ETHOS: Is that right?

CALLISTO: He likes the way lilacs fuck him.

ETHOS: The way hydrangeas fuck him.

CALLISTO: The way poppies fuck him.

ETHOS: The way honeysuckles fuck him.

CALLISTO: The way nasturtiums fuck him.

ETHOS: The way chicories fuck him.

CALLISTO: The way daisies fuck him.

ETHOS: The way morning glories fuck him.

CALLISTO: Oh fuck, fuck, fuck.

ETHOS: In a matter of a single millennium.

CALLISTO: All the fleurs want to fuck him.

ETHOS: He is one lucky bastard.

CALLISTO: Bastard he is. (*Sotto voce.*)

ETHOS: How are—

CALLISTO: When I was a kid, we used to play a game of hopscotch. When a girl jumped up, especially a girl with gaudy interiors, we would bet on how many flowers we could count on each of her butt cheeks. That was our hopscotch. It was risky, an innovative scheme. There were many complications.

ETHOS: What kind of complications?

CALLISTO: Many girls did not don *any* daedal underwear.

ETHOS: Ah, well.

CALLISTO: There was another game we played called marble golf. We would thumb a small hole in the ground. And we'd try to flick a marble into another marble to knock it into the hole. Whoever flicked the most marbles into the hole in one go was the torero.

ETHOS: I suspect the title of torero belonged to no one but you, Callisto.

CALLISTO: I was a dashing little thing. Tell me about your youth.

ETHOS: My father, as you know, died of prostate cancer. My moth—

CALLISTO: I have to tell you about this strange dream I had last
night. I thought I was online, in some kind of cyber theater.
There was a pop-up window, a dog incessantly barking, barking.
I thought if I closed the window—the window of the perpetual
dog barker—it would end the barking. I closed the window,
but the dog continued to bark. When I woke up, I found the
sound was coming from the hospital window—a dog, outside
of my vision, was barking, and its owner was yelling for it to
come. I closed the hospital window. As soon as I closed it, the
dog stopped barking. I don't believe the mind can distinguish
between the literal world and the conceptual world. What
does it mean to close the window on the internet in a dream
and to close the window in the hospital? Are they one and the
same? What is the conceptual difference? Does my mind only
know that I need to close some sort of window? Or does my
subconscious manufacture an internet screen in order to attend
to the service of the conscious world, which recognizes that a
window, virtual or nonvirtual, has to be closed? Or is my mi—
ETHOS: Callisto, I would love to hear more, but I am here for
Catholic.
CALLISTO: She's here? Why doesn't she stop—
ETHOS: She's being operated on.
CALLISTO: Dear heavens! Is she okay?
ETHOS: Fine. Perfectly fine. She's just banning all immigrants
from entering the country. Including yours.
CALLISTO: What?
ETHOS: I have to go. I don't want the emptiness of postsurgery to
ambush her.

I exit room 220 while Callisto's mouth hangs open.

CATHOLIC: Ethos! Please move the sewing machine from the blue room to the balcony!

ETHOS: Where?

CATHOLIC: To the balcony!

ETHOS: Why?

CATHOLIC: I can't breathe in the blue room.

ETHOS: But try!

CATHOLIC: I can't. Please, please Ethos. There's more air. So much more air on the balcony.

Moving the sewing machine requires that I disconnect it from the table. The last time I disassembled the sewing machine, Catholic was six months gravid with the twins. I walk into the blue room, which remains as blue and sulfuric as a blue moon can be. We haven't set foot in this room since we lost the twins. We emptied it, leaving only the sewing machine. I walk up to the machine, remove the dusty shirt covering it, and begin the mechanical task of taking it apart. I unplug the cord from the socket. The difficult part of removing the belt from the handwheel and pulley is sliding the belt back onto the pulley. I tilt the sewing machine slightly away from me to release the tension on the belt. I detach the long neck bolt under the table, and then I turn the machine on its side so it lies on the table like the head of a horse that's about to be euthanized. I lift the machine to the balcony. The entire task, which I thought would take me all morning, takes me twenty minutes.

ETHOS: Catholic!

CATHOLIC: Yes?

ETHOS: My hands are full. Can you open the screen door?

Catholic comes immediately into the kitchen. She pulls the screen door to one side, and the salt of the sea climbs its way into our nostrils. I return to the blue room and carry the table 15.3 feet to the balcony. I keep it pressed to my stomach, my arms wrapped around it like a sling. The view of the sewing machine on its table facing the sea is quiet and nostalgic. Before I have transferred all the fiberboard from the truck to the garage, she has made herself at home. She sits on a rocking chair with the sewing machine and faces the distant sea. The machine rattles along quickly, as if it has joined the Napoleonic Wars.

All Sunday evening Catholic is bent over the pinewood table, sketching over a dozen sewing patterns on colossal rolls of translucent paper. Her back aches from bending over. The patterns measure the corporeal dimensions of Pistachio and Dogfish, obtained from the fish specialist, Lorenzo Mancha. Pistachio is a scribbled angelfish: *Chaetodontoplus duboulayi*. He, at 10.1 inches, looks like an enlarged pistachio. A pistachio, in general, is only a full tongue and a jaw. The only species on the planet that exists as a jaw and a fat tongue that fills up its entire abode. Dogfish, a 13.7-inch oriental sweetlips or *Plectorhinchus vittatus*, doesn't bark and has a weakness for mollusks and serpent stars. Catholic is stitching three pairs of semi-winter outfits made with fishnet stocking fabric for Dogfish and Pistachio.

Caked in sawdust, I run the blade of the heavy-duty vertical band saw through the fiberboard in the garage. I have been at it since five in the morning. The sky is dark, brewing thunderstorms, on the brink. I measure the fiberboard and cut it into the dimensions of the aquarium base. At nine, I ascend the stairs from the basement. My wife is on her way out of the bedroom. The way she exits. The way her legs move. Scissors that cut through the hallway toward our bed. She walks toward me awkwardly as if she were walking through me. Each walk is a cut. I try to memorize her cut. As if I were studying the seam of the room. She cuts with each step. She cuts through me. My eyes try to retrieve something from between her legs. Something is hiding. Two droplets of maroon liquid descend her thighs. I throw the goggles caked in sawdust from my hands onto the floor and run to her. Her head presses against my chest.

> CATHOLIC: Ethos.
> ETHOS: Are you okay?
> CATHOLIC: I think so.
> ETHOS: Catholic. Where do you want to be? In bed? I can take you there.
> CATHOLIC: No. No. No. (*She mumbles.*)
> ETHOS: Where?
> CATHOLIC: Bathtub.

With my arms underneath her legs and torso and her right hand around my neck, I lift Catholic into the bathroom. I kick the bathroom door. It opens. She reaches out to the wall and turns on the light.

> ETHOS: Why are you bleeding?
> CATHOLIC: I wasn't expecting—
> ETHOS: Is it from the operation?
> CATHOLIC: No . . . it came early. It came so much and so violently.

The bathtub is not a riverbed, but I take her there. I set her down into it gently, her feet pressing flat against the bathtub wall. I adjust the hot and cold water nozzles so the temperature is below scorching. I cup water with my palms and release it in between her thighs. The blood writhes toward the drain from her white skirt. She stands up slowly, then grips the corners of her blouse and lifts it over her body. She aims for the bathroom sink, but it lands on the limestone countertop. I hold onto her waist. I unzip her skirt and let it fall like an opera house curtain. She sits back down in the tub.

ETHOS: Do you want the shower on?
CATHOLIC: Yes.

Water sprinkles out from the showerhead. Pellets of water step on Catholic's face, stretching and distorting her face and her eyelashes.[2] I pull the shower curtain forward to keep the water from leaping out. My head pokes inward around it. I drop the lid of the toilet and sit down on it. I stare at the alabaster tiles, naked and shining, reflecting my face. My face looks like a grocery sack floating into the foggy atmosphere of an afternoon.

I leave the bathroom. I walk around the house a bit, wondering if I should return to the carpentry job in the garage. The sharp pains circulating my stomach remind me why I ascended in the first place. I take bread from the top of the refrigerator. Toss half the loaf into the haversack and part of the other half into my mouth. I open the refrigerator door and withdraw a stick of butter. I grab a cutting board and a bread knife; I cut the stick into three equal parts. One I put in the refrigerator. Another I wrap in wax paper and toss into the haversack. The rest I spread onto the bread. I chew with all my might. When my hunger subsides, I notice a pair of pallid, pruned feet dangling on the armrest of the sofa.

My wife lies like a wound. The breeze lifts the curtain so it appears pregnant with air. The curtain flutters. I walk into the closet near the living room. I take out a blanket and throw it over her body. She sleeps as if she's tucked under a hundred thin layers of phyllo dough. I gaze at her. The urge to lick the sugar coat the nap leaves on her eyelids is

---

2. Showerheads bear a certain similarity to Box jellyfish, which have twenty-four eyes, like the showerhead. And the Box jellyfish, like the showerhead, has four parallel brains that allow it a 360-degree panoramic view of my wife's naked body.

unbearable. I kneel on the Russian rug and press my face against her stomach. My left hand lies to my side, and my right is thrown on the long highway of her thigh. Seamlessly, I drift into another world.

I dream that I am wearing a blue shirt, riding a bicycle through sand. I dream that I drop the bicycle on the beach. I dive into the cold water and drown. The way I drown seems important. I drown by entering a sunken ship. When I exit the ship, there are three sunflowers between my teeth. I grind the sunflower stems until the stems cut out the last drop of my breath. It goes somewhat like this: My teeth amputate one leg of the sunflower, and the sunflower floats up to the surface of the sea. Reality catches up with me through death. Everything is moving slowly and hexagonally as I exit the sea. Water clings to my human attire. In the thick coat of sweetened sunlight, I ride the bicycle through sand. Naturally, I am still dead.

When my eyes flutter open, my wife is still sedated in her formless monologue of a dream.

When my eyes flutter open, my wife is still sedated in her formless monologue of a dream. When my eyes flutter open, my wife is still sedated in her formless monologue of a dream. When my eyes flutter open, my wife is still sedated in her formless monologue of a dream.

This sentence replays itself over and over again in the theater of my mind. As if the disc in my head is scratched. Life is too austere and oblique to have become a broken toy so soon and so eagerly. It has grown so dark and solemn. I hear voices in her hair, which awaken me to the present moment. I realize Catholic is talking in her sleep. She even completes a sentence or two in between extensive gaps.

CATHOLIC: I—I—I c-can't sayyyyy that y-your body . . . c-can't s-s-s-spill . . . o-o-on my b-body.
ETHOS: Catholic?

I touch her shoulder, shaking her lightly.

CATHOLIC: Hmm . . .

She turns her shoulder away. I am alone again to face the wall. To face the imminent darkness. I stay still, and my wife stays still. The

blankness expands so when I face my wife again (her hair), I face everything: a long, narrow street that's pushed around by the twirling wind
of my disposable thoughts. I hear voices descending from her hair again.

CATHOLIC: Orrr . . . t-the way light-t f-falls into y-your l-l-light.
ETHOS: Catholic? Are you here?

The completeness of her sentences gives me the illusion of hope. I am
hoping that she is awake and that she is declaring to me, "Yes, although
I can't say that your body can't spill on my body. Or the way light falls
into your light. Stretch yourself to me." I'm hoping she's awake to talk
with me; to run her hands through my hair; to look at an online cata-
log of fish with me; to play Scrabble with me; to do something with
my hands or to play with my lackluster penis; to make a meal with
me; to tie my hands to a chair; to rub unguent on my back; to write a
letter to my mother with me; to cut my toenails; to climb a tree naked
with me; to do anything except lie there like a squash, ripening without
me. When I touch her, I can tell she is really asleep—sleeping deeply,
moaning—and not pretending to be asleep as I sometimes catch her
doing in the middle of the night or in the afternoon. When she pretends, her shoulders are taller and more angular, not rounded like they
are now. Even in the dark I can distinguish the roundness of her shoulder blades, the roundness of her pose. I used to love to watch her sleep,
when Colin and Abby were crawling along the walls of the house.

Everything is impossible. Her love for me, if there is any left, is
impossible. The sacrifice she made when she resuscitated me. Has it
always been a wrong choice? When the twins were here, time alone was
so rare. Any moment alone was diamonds, pure glacier. Unable to bear
myself in her presence, I remove myself from her hemisphere. I lean
back into the coffee table and raise myself up with my hands. Just like
that. In one quick and mechanical motion, I exit the diagram of her
body. The diagram of the living room. With all their narratives and
the empty lines and shadows and incomplete voices. I don't know if I
can bend for them anymore. Extend their narratives. Narratives that
no one will care to read.

I find myself in the kitchen, moving into solitary poses. All the frames in the house are still flipped inward, images facing the wall and backs exposed to the viewer. On the one in the hallway, the number *89x* is written in charcoal on flexible cardboard. Catholic refuses to let me reverse them back to their original arrangement. She threatens to file for divorce if she ever finds the frames back in their old postures. Of course, it never occurs to me to test the validity of her threat. I always view her threats in this light: at a gambling table, the house always wins. But the kings are always pretty. Too pretty. With cuffs and whiskers and proper wigs and a crown that celebrates St. Patrick's Day all year round. They have those short swords. What useless swords.

I take a bottle of Blue Moon from the refrigerator. I close the refrigerator, grab the beer opener magnetized to the front, uncap the beer, toss the cap into the sink, and walk to the screen door. I open the screen door and step onto the balcony. I stand there like a front burner gazing at the stars and the dismal, faraway sea. My circular face becomes heated as quickly as the platinum-wire coil from an electric range. It's from the impulse of chugging down an entire bottle of Blue Moon. I savor nothing. Not the air, not the air, not the moon, not the moon, and certainly not the yeast-fermented malt. I close the glass door behind me and pull the cushioned chair out from Catholic's sewing machine and sit down. I yell:

"DEAD END"

Probably no one hears me. Possibly someone does. Does it matter? Is fax paper pH neutral? How can Catholic abandon me here?

"NO STARS LEFT IN ANYONE'S HEART"

Tiredness brings me to my knees, and I find myself crawling onto the ground. Without much provocation, I fall asleep.

When my eyes crack open at the sign of the first matutinal light, Catholic is standing above me in high heels, wearing navy slacks and a red blouse. She looks like a rhubarb stalk.

CATHOLIC: Ethos, I've been looking all over for you. What are you doing out here?

ETHOS: I don't know.

CATHOLIC: I microwaved some biscuits. They're on the table. I bled on everything and slept through everything, and I have to leave right now!

ETHOS: Yes, yes, yes . . .

CATHOLIC: Are you alright?

ETHOS: Yes, yes, yes. Just go. I'll take care of it.

I hear her heels clicking and clicking. I peel myself from the wood, but my face falls back down again. The night did not freeze the soggy membranes of my head evenly. My lungs feel dislodged. On the second attempt, I lift myself awkwardly. My mind remobilizes, walking in circles from one idea to the next. My headache makes my face feel like it's floating. I wipe my face with the sleeve of my sweater. An impulse runs through my body like electricity: my children, my children. Just yesterday's teardrops. Did my daughter taste metallic? Or was it my son?

Their receding laugher encroaches as I move into the kitchen. Their neonatal claps. Their lips: sweet, glossy, and thundering. Today, I will learn to die properly. It's just a hallucination now. Nothing is real. Swinging left and right: death by hibachi. I walk toward the bedroom to look for the ropes. Virginia Woolf did it in the water with big rocks in her pockets. I simply have to sink down on land with something. With anything.

When I enter the bedroom, the sheets activate my eyes. Oh, Catholic! Death is certain. Death is certainly blooming in my mouth. The sheets are coated with dried blood, small parched ponds and big parched ponds, and then smaller blotches that trail unevenly on the EXTREMELY HIGH THREAD COUNT sheets. Was it twelve hundred, or was it fifteen? The Egyptians won't forgive Catholic for violating their army of weft and warp yarns. I rush to the fitted sheet, throw myself onto it, and tug and pull the elastic band that's tucked around each corner. I hoist it right out of its contraption. Then I throw it toward the bedroom door.

My death must be inevitably delayed (yet again!). I leap off the bed and rush to the bathroom, making sure to step over the fitted sheet and not on it. I grab a tall bottle of shampoo and the bristle brush underneath the sink and return to the bed. I squeeze two or three droplets of thyme gel onto one pond and scrub at it gently with the brush. I proceed in the same way with all the stains. On the last smear job, I gaze upward and extend that gaze as long as I am able. Out into the world framed by the window.

The clouds are turning their shoulders. Moving slowly and methodically. Yes, the morning is already long and cold and extensive. But I realize more and more as life shifts its position that I can't change the world by looking at it longer. I am writing the page of my life without adding more carbon monoxide into it or hanging myself from a synthetic rope. Life is so simple and beautiful. Why am I so quick to discard it when things are becoming more difficult, stoic, and ordinary? Was there less life when things in the past were daedal, painful, or histrionic?

Although my mind confuses eruption for euphoria and devotion for diaspora, it clearly distinguishes today from tomorrow and yesterday from today. Or does it? Perhaps it blurs yesterday and tomorrow with the present so that life is one extended breath, minced to calendric intervals. Perhaps we are fit to perform only one duty: exhaling. Perhaps in life and in language, one can substitute one word for another word like pouring water from one glass into another. And perhaps I would like to surrogate exhaling for a more fitting dualistic jab: expiring.[3]

I gaze back down at the floral mattress. Raw, germ-ridden, bug-infested white floral mattress exposed to air. The pillows, like large, bleached raviolis, are the only immaculate objects in the vicinity. Even though they are on the verge of sainthood, ready to be crowned for their cherubic cleanliness, I seize the pair of them and toss them on the oak chest at the foot of the bed. I peel the comforter from the flat sheet and push it onto the floor. I lift the languishing flat sheet from its position and toss it toward the bedroom door. I stare at the thyme-scented ponds. There is a gloss, a lovely gloss, on the mattress top. I am almost tempted to bend down and kiss it.

On my knees on the mattress, I begin to scrub the macerated ponds with all my might. Rosy foam rises from their froth and curls onto the

---

3. The binary biological and ontological nature of the word *expiring* has two obvious unfoldings. First, it informs me of its paradoxical complex, and second, it provokes me (though I am not going to do this now) to walk to the yogurt container or the milk jug searching for dates. *Expiring* appears to symbolize life the most closely. How could a word that means both breathing (exhaling air from the lungs) and coming to an end (death) not satisfy my philosophical needs? I stare at the clouds some more. For things that don't say much and move very slowly, they seem to spew a lot of foam and air. Perhaps they are trying to say something.

seabed. The sea comes back to me on the landmass of the mattress. Perhaps the children will return as I shift the rudder of the brush. I can see the sea-foam crashing against the brush's hull. Perhaps, at the bottom of this sea depth, mattress depth, the surface of the mattress, there is an entire civilization of sea life waiting for me on its aquatic deck. Perhaps, and perhaps so much more. I hop over the sheets, retrieve a towel from the bathroom, and return to the bed.

I sweep and scrape the foam onto the towel, trying to find its bottom. I expect rainbow fish, blobfish, lobsters, sponges, sea stars, anglerfish, leafy sea dragons, cartilaginous fish, longhorn cowfish, anemones, frilled sharks, crabs, vampire squid, octopi, viperfish, seahorses, minnows, seashells, axolotls, eels, and stargazers, but only find a faint, oh-so-faint 7.3 millimeters of thin, pink, diaphanous salmon flesh on the seafloor of the mattress. I can't even peel it off to sample it. For taste and pleasure.

I pull myself off the mattress so the air can dry it. I stroll back into the bathroom and situate the towel, shampoo bottle, and brush on the counter. I return to the bedroom and separate the stained sheet from the unstained. With the stained sheet bundled in one hand and the unstained in the other, I reenter the bathroom. I throw the fitted sheet into the bathtub and the flat sheet on the travertine floor. I grab the brush and lower the cover of the toilet seat and sit on it. I turn the cold spigot of the faucet on and wet the sheet just a little before quickly shutting it off. I turn around, retrieve the bottle of thyme shampoo, and place it on the ledge of the tub.

My hands flounder in search of the stains. When I finally find them, I grab the bottle and squirt some on the stains and try to bend forward to scrub them out. It's awkward and difficult. What to do? I go to the kitchen, pull out a cutting board, and take it back to the bathroom. I sit down on the toilet seat, place the cutting board on my lap, and pull the dampened sheets on top of the board. I begin to scrub with the brush. A mixture of water and shampoo spits outwardly, hitting the hair on my arms. I do not care where the spitting lands as long as the floral mucilage is exonerated. I work hard, calmly and methodically. I sat in this same position with Colin bent over my thighs, scrubbing chili stains from his butt cheeks.

Catholic had set a pot of chili on the kitchen floor because the table and the counter were covered with Thanksgiving leftovers. She had wanted to make room in the refrigerator for all the uneaten food and the pot of chili. Instead of putting the chili in his mouth like any other three-year-old would have, he crawled over and sat his naked ass in it.

Tears overflow my eyes and drip onto the sheets, mixing with the shampoo, foam, and Catholic's menstrual pigment. I continue to brush blindly; the gossamer veil of the tears obstructs my vision of the sheets but not my movement. Mucus from my nose drips into the liquid mixture. I drive the brush back and forth, thinking the sheet is a coffin or two, trying to sand until there's not a single fiber of wood left. Not even the powdery substance of sawdust. The brush strokes rush in and out of the air until my arm becomes tired. And then, I stop. I stop and wipe my tears and mucus on the upper part of my shirtsleeve. I grab the sheet. When I stand up, the cutting board flops off my thighs and falls on the floor. It makes a flapping sound like the bellies of two elephant seals colliding. I bend over the tub, plug the drain, throw the fitted sheet in, and then pick up the flat one and throw it in as well. I twist the hot and cold spigots and exit the bathroom.

I descend to the basement for Charlie's Soap Powder and a plastic laundry basket. I pour one-third pound of powdered detergent into the tub and stir the mixture with my hands. When the sheets are fully soaped, I unplug the drain, let the water run out, and then fill the tub back up. I lift the sheets in the air, dip them back down again, and go through the motion a dozen times. I drain and refill the tub again. I explore the sheets thoroughly to see if I can relocate the stains, but I can't find any. It must be difficult to see different shades when the fabric is wet. I wrench the sheets as tightly as my muscles allow and throw them in the laundry basket. Once, in bed, Catholic told me her uterus during menstruation was like a laundry machine: "The washer-uterus uses hydraulics to twist and untwist the uterine lining, trying to shred the endometrium out. It does a regular laundry cycle[4] every twenty-eight days or so."

I teased her afterward: "Where to look when confronted with a missing sock?"

I wrench the water from the flat sheet and toss it into the basket. I carry the basket outside into the backyard. I walk up to the clothesline and unclip four wooden clothespins and stuff them into my jeans pocket. I grab one of the sheets, untwist it, and toss it up onto the clothesline. I spread the sheet out so it extends from one end of the line to the other, then I begin clipping the clothespins to the sheet. The morning air is brisk like biscuits. The biscuits Catholic microwaved! Something to look forward to after this, I think.

The backyard is soundless, not a bird in sight. I scan my neighbors' yards. What my mother said is true: one can't be depressed if one is engaged in physical activity. How can I possibly return to suicide after

---

4. Eco-anthropologists have theorized about the energy conservation of reconstructing the uterine hut every fecund cycle. Some mammals absorb the huts in their bodies instead of shedding them. That's a lot of huts to collect in one year—more than stamps! My wife is very fortunate to not have to carry all those huts around. In fact, uterus specialist Beverly Strassmann suggests that perhaps it costs more energy-wise to do continuous upkeep on the hut than it does to have it demolished. I think her reasoning skills are quite advanced. So reasonable. Who would want to live in a hut no one can crawl into just because it's there? But more importantly, who wants to live in an apartment when it might be bulldozed the next day? Temporary living arrangements are always sketchy and not to be trusted. I can't be sentimental, either. I used to live in apartment 7A, but the landlord destroyed it. It must be because I failed to scrub the left compartment of the refrigerator thoroughly. It must be that nine-month, dried-out mustard clump I couldn't seem to scour completely with my newly developed extremities. It had to go. And although you can't see the apartment where I used to live, at least I can point you to where the lot is. Just imagine what it was like before it was flattened. Just imagine. Indoor trellis. A swimming pool. And even though you couldn't run around in it, a small backyard. Plenty of free food dropping from the sky. And, on top of that, I even had a live-in butler or butlet or bullet or whatever, but whenever I ring that bell, or rather, pull that cord, man oh man, the driver always stops for me, and I always get what I want. Generally, it comes in the form of free dairy products (false advertisement!) and always sauerkraut! What is with the sauerkraut?

this? And homicide couldn't possibly exist if criminals did laundry by hand. This is why prison systems work so well: the prisoners wash shirts and sheets in bulk in steamy warehouses and fold them into rectangles and insert them into colossal linen bins. One must return to the ordinary for salvation.

After the flat sheet, I proceed to the fitted sheet. This one is harder. Its elastic band makes it difficult to stretch without jerking the clothesline around. In the middle of clipping, Lidia calls out to me from her yard.

LIDIA: Callisto and I would like you and Catholic to come over for dinner next week. Will you be able to make it?

I turn my body toward her, holding the basket against my hip.

ETHOS: I don't know. I'll have to talk to Catholic. You know how these things go.

LIDIA: Sure.

ETHOS: How are you?

LIDIA: Great!

ETHOS: Good.

LIDIA: Actually, I came out here because Callisto wanted me to ask if your wife has read his letter yet?

ETHOS: I don't know.

LIDIA: Can't you ask her?

ETHOS: She's at work.

LIDIA: Can you call her?

ETHOS: Sure, give me just a moment. Is it that important?

LIDIA: Well, Callisto has been harassing me all morning about it. And I just want to get it over with, you know?

ETHOS: Certainly. Let me go inside for a second. I'll let you know.

Inside, I dial Catholic's number. The phone rings, but there's no answer. She must be out of her office. I'm about to leave a message when—

CATHOLIC: Ms. Romulus speaking.
ETHOS: Catholic, it's Ethos.
CATHOLIC: Yes. Is it urgent?
ETHOS: Very urgent, for Callisto.
CATHOLIC: What is it?
ETHOS: Have you read the letter he wrote you?
CATHOLIC: Which letter?
ETHOS: The one I left on the kitchen counter.
CATHOLIC: Oh, that one.
ETHOS: Well?
CATHOLIC: Yes.
ETHOS: Was it romantic?
CATHOLIC: . . .
ETHOS: Catholic?
CATHOLIC: Somewhat.
ETHOS: Oh, I see.

There is an absence of sound. Three to four seconds.

ETHOS: Will I see you at home tonight?

CATHOLIC: Very late.

ETHOS: Oh.

CATHOLIC: Did you eat the biscuits?

ETHOS: Not yet, looking forward to it.

CATHOLIC: Ethos, I have to get back to work. Bye.

The thing about suicide is, it's a very selfish act. This is why it should only be done once in a lifetime. I reheat the cold biscuits, sit in the chair, and eat while crying. Did she really choose me over the children? Or was it by chance, not a choice for her at all? If the logic was that I was irresistible, meaning irreplaceable, then to choose my survival over theirs meant that they could easily be rehatched, so to speak. This inadvertently suggests that I could not be rehatched, or be rehatched that easily. But this is such absurd, backward logic.

Lidia is complicit with the affair. I am complicit with it too, in some distorted way. Guilt is the culprit of justification. There must be something extraordinary about the migration of emotions, about trying to find a livable home for the body in a new land, even if that new land is acrid and broken as a tailbone. The morning passes her hand over to the afternoon, a brief hello, and there is the afternoon waiting on a plate before me. In the darkness of my contemplation, the sun emerges.

I walk to the kitchen chair where the haversack slouches. I begin to pour its contents out onto the kitchen table. Bread crumbs fall on the table like snowflakes. There are a few receipts, three butter cubes wrapped in wax paper, a fountain pen, and two medium-sized chunks of dehydrated French bread. The bread bounces on the table like the skull of a bird. I smooth out the receipts. My eyes scan their inventories. They are receipts, faintly yellow, for the fiberboard, nails, and other items I purchased the same day I ordered the glass. I wonder if the glass is ready. I walk to the phone book lying on top of the refrigerator. I take it down and crack it open and flip through the pages. I find Sella Windows in the business section. I grab the phone from the kitchen counter and dial the number. The phone rings. A feminine voice comes forth from the earpiece like a bird perching on an electrical wire.

CLERK: Sella Windows.
ETHOS: I'm wondering if my order has arrived?
CLERK: What's your last name?
ETHOS: Romulus.
CLERK: One moment, please.

I press the phone against my ear with my shoulder. I put the phone book back on top of the refrigerator. I stare out at the yard, at the way the light coats everything with a thin layer of butter. I gaze at the sheets on the clothesline: a beautiful segment of my wife's past is dissolving, dispersing through the sheets. I feel them there for the time being. For the time being, the sadness swells in my chest. Everything is beginning to make sense. Except my cheekbone has started to hurt, and I simply do not know why. The world is opening up. I laugh now when I shouldn't laugh. When I'm still on the phone.

When the light is this substantial, the world becomes clearer. This world made of light and darkness, of beauty and ruin, so incapable of apocalypse. The device life is designed on, an earth so round and verdant and polluted, is good. The fear of today's youth is not annihilation, but that life will continue after destruction. The aftermath is more terrifying than the collision. When things are moving that quickly, one can't feel—

CLERK: I'm so sorry to keep you waiting, but your items haven't arrived yet. By ground, shipments always take longer.

ETHOS: Thanks for checking.

CLERK: Gladly. We'll give you a call when they get here. Let me verify the phone number we have on file . . .

Hungry and not wanting to do anything about it, I stroll slowly to the sofa and sit down. Time elapses, and eventually, in the absence of sound, I fall into a nap.

In the cool of evening, I drive Catholic to the ocean. We walk along the coastline. A big ship honks in the middle of the sea. Sailboats flutter to and fro, afraid of being flattened by the big ship like angelfish. Last summer we brought a dozen fish here from the artificial habitat of our tank. Today we are empty-handed. Orion is still pinned up to the sky. We walk and don't talk and walk and walk, even when our legs feel like they're going to fall off, even when it becomes too dark to see our own footsteps, even when we're drenched in sweat. The odor of the marsh, of our bladders working too hard. There are no public restrooms until eleven blocks from here, at a dinky bar that leans left. We are walking from the grainy sand on hard, bituminous asphalt. The way night is unwinding compels me to activate my vocal cords. And in a seamless mood, Rafael Alberti's canción "Si mi voz muriera en tierra . . ." lifts the glottis in my throat and I vibrate into the night:

Si   mi   voz   muriera   en   tierra,
llevadla   al   nivel   del   mar
y   dejadla   en   la   ribera.

Llevadla		al	nivel	del	mar
y		nombradla			capitana
de	un	blanco	bajel	de	guerra.

¡Oh	mi	voz	condecorada
con	la	insignia	marinera:

sobre	el	corazón	un	ancla
y	sobre	el	ancla	una	estrella
y	sobre	la	estrella	el	viento
y	sobre	el	viento	la	vela!

My bare feet stroll the sand bed. My wife is far away from me, her elegant form walking closer to the large black rocks caked in moss and algae. As I walk toward her, almost near her, I contemplate the sand. It overlaps the rocks and jettisoned artifacts: seashells, crab legs, broken beer bottles. Are we made of mud or sand? If we are made of sand, do we burn up from the inside rather quickly, like a kiln? Or do we emerge from the kiln like glass jars? We must be made of sand; it's the only way to rationalize how quickly our realities disintegrate. In hell, everyone becomes glass. Or ceramic plates.

> *Dear Rome,*
> My wife and I can't be with you at the Colosseum. Our greetings to Vespasian. Do tell me, though, why glass can't expand.
> *Ethos*

The night is sipping all the tea along the coastline. A pile of polychromatic leaves curls and dances on the asphalt as we come closer to the electric lights. The wind lifts them and drops them like puppets on strings. They roll and tumble into one another. The children of autumn. I want to bundle them up in my arms and take them to a ballet class. The wind also lifts the short skirts of the college girls in front of us. The skirts swing high and low like a matador's cape. If the wind were a bull, these girls would have been gored by now. The curves of their nubile thighs. The thin, transparent fabric of their tights. The backs of their pumps digging into their skin. These young neophytes of Dionysus. Children of autumn. How I want to bundle them up in my arms and dress them in wool top to bottom. I turn to my wife to gauge her reaction to these hypothermia-induced, translucent sylphs. She is lost in her own thoughts. The strong hands of the wind are braiding her hair, blowing her pheromones around.

My wife climbs into bed after an evening along the coastline. She comes to bed not as a gown, but as a window into which I climb. Through the bedroom window, I see Lidia and Callisto's kitchen. I see a painting and two chairs. When I turn my face to look through my wife (the window), I see the shimmering, undulating sea. My vision is not an insight. It is literature I stuff into her flesh. It doesn't belong there. In the darkness, I have craved light. From the window, I see the half-moon riding on electrical wires. I walk far from the oven. Stand closer to the balcony, where the sewing machine sits. I wait for my body to return to the window, my wife.

In the morning, my wife closes her shutters. She yawns. I reach out to touch her soft skin. She appears less like a mausoleum. The beginning of foreplay, perhaps. We have been living together almost like brother and sister. When I touch her, it seems incestuous. Usually, she withdraws. This morning too, she withdraws: her skin shifts and her shoulders shift. Her shutters are closed to light and to my hands. I lean to my side, my hand bent, elbow digging into the sheets, palm supporting my head, and facing her, I play with the lace on her evening gown, which during the tossing and turning of the night has shifted significantly upward. Perhaps my wife has priapic amnesia. A medical condition in which she forgets (often!) that I have a penis. Or perhaps it's the reverse; perhaps I have clitoral amnesia. In which case, shall I remind myself that she has one? This is a challenging puzzle, perhaps like sudoku. The grids of sudoku bring to mind another logic problem. My wife's reproductive organs may simply be one of hundreds of lockers at a gym. And my strenuous efforts to turn the dial, to try different combinations, may not open her locker. Suppose I do decode the cryptic language of her desire. What if I break into that miniature compartment only to find an old pair of tennis shoes? What will I do then?

In November, morning glories are difficult to find, but Catholic has planted the silent, iridescent trumpets in pots along the kitchen window-sill. When the wind howls from the north, the glass rattles against the pots. My bones shift in my body like stones bursting forth into the riverbed. When we walk to the sea, my wife likes to pluck the morning glories from the breaths of their matutinal aria and tuck them inside her bra. "No currency is as rich as morning glories," she says, securing them in her cups.

I was in the garage at five in the morning, making miniature caskets out of fiberboard and nails. The caskets are three-by-seven inches and two inches deep. Their lids slide on and off.

In the kitchen, the teapot comes to a hissing boil. I grip the handle and lift the pot from the gas range and empty the boiling water into two teacups, a bag of African rooibos in each one. The teacups wait on the table while I flip through the pages of the newspaper. I put down the newspaper and grab a spoon from the saucer. I lift the paper tag on the teabag and place it on the spoon, then wrap the white string around the teabag and spoon five times. I squeeze the rest of the liquid into the teacup, then I unwind the string and drop the teabag onto the plate. I pour a bit of whole milk into the cup and carry it out to the balcony. Catholic sits on the chair wearing a shearling jacket with thick wool cuffs. I can't imagine how she's able to press the fabric through the needle plate without her cuffs getting in the way.

ETHOS: Tea, Catholic?
CATHOLIC: No.

ETHOS: Try some; it's packed with antioxidants and relieves
    nervous tension.
CATHOLIC: But I'm not nervous.

I carry the teacup back into the kitchen and place it on the counter. I
think she has declined it because the tea lacks chocolate almond biscotti.
I'm taking the tin of biscotti down from the cabinet when the doorbell
chimes. I walk to the door and open it, smiling.

ETHOS: Good to see you. Come on in.
LIDIA: Hi, Ethos!
ETHOS: Would you like some rooibos tea with chocolate almond
    biscotti?
LIDIA: Oh yes! Of course.
ETHOS: I've just made some for Catholic. Would you like to join
    her on the balcony?

She's in the middle of sewing three outfits.

LIDIA: I'd love to.
ETHOS: How's Callisto?
LIDIA: He's getting better. He came home from the hospital
    today.

I pull a chair from the kitchen table and carry it to the balcony.

ETHOS: Lidia is here, Catholic.
CATHOLIC: Tell her to come out.
LIDIA: I'm practically right behind you, Catholic.

I balance biscotti and two cups of tea on a tray. I place the tray on an
iron table that used to be a plant stand.

LIDIA: I hope the pending winter doesn't scare us into nival
    oblivion.
CATHOLIC: The north comes, with salt and tears.
LIDIA: As does the wind from the south.
ETHOS: I have winter in my heart.

CATHOLIC: How's Callisto?

LIDIA: I don't know. I want to get away from him. There's
something about his garrulous lips. They almost seem to quiver,
like the mouth of a bird before winter arrives.

I pleasantly and diplomatically excuse myself from the women and
reenter the kitchen. I feel safer here, away from the tabloid. Most jellyfish lack digestive, central nervous, or osmoregulatory systems. They
have no need for lungs; their skin is so filmy and flimsy that their bodies are oxygenated by diffusion. I walk over to the chair near the din-
ing room table and lift my coat off its back. I put my coat on and throw
the haversack over my body. I stare at the morning glories lining the
windows. They're wilting. I walk over to them and cut their stems with
scissors until there are a dozen white and purple morning glories in the
palm of my hand.

I descend the stairs and make my way into the garage. The fall air cuts
through me. I walk over to the caskets on the sawdust-covered vertical
band saw and place the morning glories on the metal toolbox. I begin
to sand one of the caskets. I finish sanding one, then pick up the other
and do the same. The bleak, pseudo-arctic air recedes from my aware-
ness as I polish the splinters off the caskets. Time seems to float in and
out of my hand. In and out of my jacket. In and out of my body. I place
the pair of receptacles on the second shelf of the garage wall and slide off
each lid. I remove the morning glories from the toolbox and carry them
to the shelf. I stack morning glories in each casket, their trumpets all
pointing the same direction. The petals become makeshift pillowcases.

I remove the haversack from my chest and poke inside so the zipper automatically slips down along the lining. I dig in and pull out two
jellyfish that look more and more like Martian candies. I place the twin
jellyfish in one sarcophagus. I lift one jellyfish from the body of the
other and deposit its head gently on the morning glory pillowcase in
the sarcophagus. I go through the same procedure for the other jellyfish. When they have been positioned inside properly, I push the lids in
till they cannot be pushed further.

Outside the garage, the wind is still howling. Carrying the coffins in one hand and the shovel in the other, I walk up to the cypress tree in the backyard. I place the coffins on the grass and begin to dig two holes (four inches by eight inches and four inches deep). The ground is hard and it's difficult. With effort, the mound of dirt accumulates into a pile. I lean the shovel against the cypress and lift the coffins and lower them into the dug-up ground. I push the dirt back over the coffins and pad it evenly. When I stand up, I notice Catholic and Lidia are watching me. I feel like a parsnip, raw and uprooted from the earth.

GARLIC

The doorbell rings, and Ethos and Catholic are nowhere in sight. I open the door to the familiar faces of Callisto and Lidia.

> CHARLEEN: You brought quiche! Thank you. How are you, Lidia? Callisto?
> CALLISTO: Wonderful.

He winks at me. I shift my gaze toward the curtain.

> LIDIA: Fall. Fall. The birds are blowing their trumpets as they begin to migrate down south.
> CHARLEEN: Yes, every morning something is always blowing its horn.
> LIDIA: How long are you visiting?
> CHARLEEN: Only a few days.
> LIDIA: That's a shame. Your winter break doesn't last a month in England?
> CHARLEEN: No, I'm just passing through for a book tour. Anne Carson and I are secretly in competition. You know, she and I are both classics professors.

LIDIA: If Anne Carson had a daughter, do you think she would name her Cardaughter?
CALLISTO: Where is Catholic?
LIDIA: Is she out in the yard?
CALLISTO: I don't see her.
LIDIA: What changed, Charleen?
CHARLEEN: Nothing has.

Thousands of garlic bulbs occupy the kitchen table. Some have cracked open. Flaky, white skins float on the table like feather lotuses.

LIDIA: What's up with all these garlic heads?
CHARLEEN: They're for planting. Want to help me crack them open?
LIDIA: I'd love to help out. No wonder you look like an angel shedding its wings.

Callisto walks to the balcony. He spots Ethos and Catholic moving up and down on the grass.

CALLISTO: They're digging up the garden bed!
LIDIA: Isn't it very late for planting? Won't the ground be too hard?
CHARLEEN: It's not too hard yet. Garlic must only be planted in the fall so it can sleep through the winter and wed the soil in spring. They're going to plant one hundred seventy cloves.
LIDIA: What for?
CALLISTO: They're trying to get rich.
LIDIA: Really? They're starting a garlic farm?
CHARLEEN: No, Lidia. It's for nourishment and health. They just have to decide if they want to plant Inchelium Red or Carpathian. One is a hard neck and the other soft.
LIDIA: But what does garlic have to do with mourning?
CHARLEEN: Why don't you sit down and I'll get you some tea? This may be a long story.

Lidia and Callisto pull the chairs from the table and sit. Their attention falls on my mouth.

CHARLEEN: So, who knows who Demeter was?

CALLISTO: Something to do with centimeters, millimeters? A type of measurement?

LIDIA: She asked *who*! Who, Callisto!

CALLISTO: Well, then, Demeter was a woman who measured hips. Where's my tea?

CHARLEEN: Not quite. Demeter was the goddess of grain and wheat. She oversaw the cultivation of the earth. She was the daughter of Cronus and Rhea.

LIDIA: Who were they?

CHARLEEN: Cronus and Rhea were brother and sister, but that's not important here. What's important is that Demeter had a daughter named Persephone.

CALLISTO: Man, if only Apple named the iPhone Persephone. It's so much sexier.

LIDIA: No one wants to hear "I want a Persephone," or "Call my Persephone," or "I have to upgrade my Persephone." It just sounds silly.

CALLISTO: Well, it isn't any different from calling a ship Alicia or a Jaguar Sweet Dolly.

CHARLEEN: Do you want to hear this story or do you want to go and help Ethos with the soil bed?

LIDIA: Yes, the daughter. Persephone, you were saying. Hey, I got distracted by Callisto's rant, but if Rhea and Cronus were brother and sister, doesn't that mean they had an incestuous fling?

CHARLEEN: It wasn't just a fling. They were married.

LIDIA: Oh my God.

CALLISTO: Not a fairy tale.

LIDIA: Definitely not a fairy tale.

CHARLEEN: So, summer used to be the only season. You could harvest all year long. Ripe fruits and vegetables: squash, cucumber, parsnip, eggplant, pumpkin, okra. There was no such thing as winter. Winter never touched the lips of earth. Until Hades came along.

CALLISTO: I know who he is.

LIDIA: God of the underworld.

CALLISTO: You two are always eating my words. You take them before I can even bite into them.

LIDIA: Sorry, Charleen. Tell us about Hades. He sounds shady.

CHARLEEN: Well, he was. In some ways. Demeter and her daughter, Persephone, along with the rest of the world, were enjoying a very extended summer. Then Hades, with his voracious appetite for petite things, noticed Persephone dancing in a wheat field and snatched her from under her mother's nose. He took her into his underworld and raped her.

LIDIA: That's just horrible. I can understand if you're craving something and you want to take it temporarily to make the hunger go away, but did he really have to rape her?

CALLISTO: He shouldn't have kidnapped her in the first place. It's such a strange word, don't you think? *Kidnap.* Like you're just taking the kid with you for a nap. At any rate, it's never okay.

LIDIA: How old was she, Charleen?

CHARLEEN: I don't know. Fairly young. Twelve. Fifteen. Sixteen. Twenty-five. Two hundred. It's all relative. When Hades took Persephone with him, Demeter roamed the earth endlessly in search of her daughter. She cried day and night. The fields were flooded with her tears. Nothing could grow in the marshy terrain. And because nothing could grow, famine struck. The whole world succumbed to Demeter's grief. Under that umbrella of darkness, the whole world starved. Nothing could grow, so there was nothing to eat.

LIDIA: Sounds like someone I know.

CHARLEEN: The earthlings began to wail to Zeus for help. Zeus tried to ignore their wailing, but he couldn't ignore it forever. He approached Demeter: "Hey, sis. What's going on here?

Why aren't you harvesting! Everyone is starving. You can't keep going like this." "Oh, brother," she said. "Our other brother, the unruly one, holds my daughter hostage in his dark world and rapes her. I miss her so much!"

LIDIA: That's awful. Who rapes his niece?

CALLISTO: Everyone does nowadays. It's a cultural thing. If you don't participate, you aren't human.

Lidia rolls her eyes.

LIDIA: Oh please, Callisto. You think the whole world is evil. Charleen, what did Zeus do?

CHARLEEN: Well, Zeus naturally felt trapped. He sympathized with his sister but couldn't quite understand his brother's behavior. He didn't believe the whole thing was being done out of mere maliciousness. After all, Hades couldn't be all evil when it came to family. So Zeus suggested to Demeter that the three of them have a nice, calm meeting to resolve the quagmire.

CALLISTO: Does Demeter tear Hades to pieces when they come together?

CHARLEEN: Well, you'll soon find out.

LIDIA: I bet she does.

CHARLEEN: When they convened, Demeter threw herself at Hades. She grabbed ahold of his black collar and nearly yanked his shirt off. She pulled his black curly hair as hard as she could. Zeus jumped in and separated them. He dropped his thunderbolt and put his hand out like a referee to keep Demeter from ripping Hades's head off.

> DEMETER: Where is my daughter, asshole?

CHARLEEN: Hades is fuming with silence.

> DEMETER: WHERE IS MY DAUGHTER, ASSHOLE?
> ZEUS: Damnit, brother. Answer her!
> HADES: She's safe at my place. I made an elaborate throne

for her in my basement. She's down there sleeping like Snow White.

DEMETER: I want Persephone back!

HADES: Well, you see, I already made her my wife.

DEMETER: You DIDN'T! She couldn't have approved! I bet you drugged her before you married her.

HADES: Come on, now! Zeus, how can you just stand by while I'm speared with false accusations?

ZEUS: Just tell us what happened. What did you do?

HADES: What did I do? Whose side are you on? You mean, what did Persephone do? All I did was put a plate of fruit out in her bedchamber. I told her she could eat all the grapes and strawberries she wanted. The moment she touched a pomegranate, though, she would automatically accept my marriage proposal. Well, Persephone ate not just one, but two hundred pomegranates.

CHARLEEN: Demeter leaped into the imaginary circle Zeus had created to separate them. She went for Hades's eyes with her fingernails.

DEMETER: You manipulated my daughter! She was probably starving. She probably hadn't eaten for days or months! You gave her no choice.

HADES: What do you mean I gave her no choice? I gave her plenty of choices. I fed her grapes and strawberries. What else would she want? The pomegranates were her own choice.

DEMETER: No wonder she ate two hundred of them. There's hardly any flesh on the seeds. She must have been famished. What have you done?

HADES: What have I done? Persephone, my lovely niece, wanted to be my bride. She was wide awake for the entire commitment thing. I made her this really beautiful ring out of dead people's skin. She seems to love it.

DEMETER: He manipulated her. I know that condition. The one where the victim sympathizes with the captor ...

ZEUS: Stockholm syndrome.

DEMETER: Yes, that must be it. My daughter has suffered so much. I want her back immediately! Zeus, command him!

ZEUS: Come on, brother. You've had your fun. Return the goods to the right owner like a good brother.

HADES: This is so absurd! Who does this? Marry the wife and return the wife to the mother? Do you see how silly this really is?

ZEUS: I do see where you are coming from, but Demeter can't live without her daughter. You have to understand this.

HADES: I love her, Zeus! She's all I have. It's so lonely down there. In that basement that never seems to stop expanding. She keeps me company. She sings and her gorgeous voice makes my whole cave vibrate. It's like being in a Béla Tarr film day and night. Also, she's an excellent cook. Brother, she can cook. It's like a festival down there. Banquets and film screenings left and right. Of course, the only film we watch in the underworld is *Satantango*. I had no idea this woman could make me so happy.

ZEUS: She's just a child.

HADES: She's not a child anymore. Please, please, please, Zeus. I beg you. Don't take her away from me.

DEMETER: Don't let him manipulate you, Zeus! His tongue is slick as ice!

ZEUS: I don't think he's trying to manipulate anyone. He truly loves her, Demeter.

DEMETER: Oh my God! He has you too! Oh my God. You've got Stockholm syndrome as well! What am I to do?

CALLISTO: Hang on a second here, Zeus took Hades's side?

CHARLEEN: Naturally, Zeus is torn apart by his brother's and sister's conflicting desires. Lidia, Callisto, what would you do in that position?

CALLISTO: I would just let Demeter and Hades sort it out on their own.

LIDIA: You're such a coward. Never picking sides, always treading on safe ground.

CALLISTO: Hey, watch it.

LIDIA: What would you do, Charleen?

CHARLEEN: My natural impulse would be to side with Demeter. She's wheat and she feeds us. It's never wise to bite the hand that feeds. And also, I sympathize with her. No one wants to deal with a rapist. Especially not when the rapist happens to love her daughter and also happens to be her brother. Conflict within a family is so difficult to resolve. And Hades, how could anyone blame him? He was born to dominate and violate. Born to take what was not his. So when he found something he wanted, it was only natural for him to obtain it through the swiftest means. Isn't violence so close to the border of death? That reminds me—today is Flannery O'Connor's birthday.

LIDIA: No kidding. How old would she be if she were still alive?

CHARLEEN: Ninty-one years old. Hades loved her Savannah flesh. Took her when she was real lupus and young.

LIDIA: Oh!

CALLISTO: So how did Zeus resolve it?

CHARLEEN: Through a compromise.

> ZEUS: I am your brother. Let's talk it out. Can't you two share custody of little Perse? During the weekdays, she'll live with you, Demeter, and on the weekends, she'll stay with Hades.
>
> DEMETER: Hades is not my husband, Zeus! He is my brother. And we're not going through a divorce, dividing

a child into two. Can't you use King Solomon as a model?
He didn't do it this way. He returned the child fully to
her mother. Can't you do something like that? I want my
child to myself! I can't negotiate the nonnegotiable.

ZEUS: That child was only a month old! He couldn't speak.
It's not the same, sister. Persephone has a mind of her own.

HADES: I shouldn't have to share my wife with her mother.

ZEUS: I think my niece should have a say in this. Retrieve
her, Hades. Quickly!

CHARLEEN: In a flash, Hades descended into his chthonic
dwelling and escorted Persephone up to earth. They arrived
before Zeus and Demeter like two flickering lightbulbs.

PERSEPHONE: Mom!
DEMETER: Persephone! My child!

CHARLEEN: Persephone and her mother embraced. There was
much weeping. Finally, Demeter spoke.

DEMETER: I want to talk to my daughter alone!

CHARLEEN: Hades whispered something to Zeus: "She's going
to brainwash her. She's going to turn her against me." Hades
walked nervously from one tree to another. Zeus quietly
advised Hades not to distrust their sister and to let things
unfold. Demeter and Persephone strolled along the edge of the
earth, arms linked.

DEMETER: Oh, I've missed you so much, daughter. Are
you well?
PERSEPHONE: It's so good to see you again. I'm wonderful,
Mother.
DEMETER: Oh, sweetheart, how could you be? I heard he
raped you.
PERSEPHONE: Mother, that was a long time ago.

DEMETER: Six months is not a long time. You mustn't take your uterus lightly. Did you use the wheat as a brush to clean it out like I showed you?

PERSEPHONE: There's no wheat in Hades's dominion, Mother.

DEMETER: That's right. Well, you can do it now that you're back on the surface.

PERSEPHONE: Hades makes an excellent brush too. He dusts the ceiling and cleans my floor. It's quite pleasurable. I just unfurl in the dark and let Father Nature do the work. I had no idea domestic life could be so fun!

DEMETER: PERSEPHONE!

PERSEPHONE: I know I lost my virginity in an unusual way, but it happened. And I am learning to move on. I know women imagine their first romance will be less or perhaps more than what I experienced. But I am your daughter, after all. And if I'm a part of you, wheat and all, and if I am part wheat, half of my body is rising to you, and the other half is entombed in the soil. And the soil is where I reside with Hades.

DEMETER: How you have grown. Yes, darling. I know my brother. I know his dark side and the nether regions of his soul. I just want you, daughter, my beloved daughter, to experience tenderness before ecstasy. Youth before necessity. Desire before infancy. Longing before nostalgia. The passage of time can't be reversed. I don't want you to miss out on the rites of womanhood and love.

PERSEPHONE: I'm experiencing all of that, Mother, and so much more!

DEMETER: You are too young to know what you haven't experienced.

PERSEPHONE: But I am experiencing it all, Mother.

DEMETER: And how is the marriage?

PERSEPHONE: We're incredibly naughty and fervent.

DEMETER: You and Hades, you—

PERSEPHONE: Yes, Mother. We fuck a lot. All the time, in fact. There's so much space down there to fuck. Any place could be used for fucking. Darkness is a virtue, you know.

DEMETER: It's overrated. He's brainwashed you. He has turned you, my little sunshine, into a gothic lover! And you are so deep in it you mistake violence for tenderness.

PERSEPHONE: Please, Mother. It's so good to see you. But I can't bear to see you like this.

DEMETER: He kidnapped and raped you! I can't get that out of my mind! And I can't even convince my daughter there's something wrong with this picture!

PERSEPHONE: Mother. Please.

DEMETER: Please, what?

PERSEPHONE: Look, I don't have a lot of choice in the matter. I could choose to be his victim or his wife. I have chosen to be his wife. He's good to me. He has sent out an army of servants to retrieve anything, and I mean *anything*, I want. Don't you see? I don't bend to his will. He bends to mine.

DEMETER: Love is not will, darling! Love is anything but will.

PERSEPHONE: I've loved him. I crave him, Mother. It's a will of some kind.

DEMETER: Yes. Yes, a will. A *willingness* to violate your ontological self. You lose your humanity when you let yourself be violated like this, darling! Don't you see?

PERSEPHONE: Mother. I see. I see that if you continue to carry on like this, you'll drive yourself mad. I must get back to my husband. He's probably anxious.

DEMETER: Yes. Of course.

CHARLEEN: They walked back on the edge of the earth, arms no longer linked.

LIDIA: Persephone is so stubborn. She makes me sick.

CALLISTO: It's not a bad thing. She has a mind of her own, and she knows how to capitalize on it!

LIDIA: Love has made her blind!

CALLISTO: Blind! That's so trite. Little women like you often confuse self-confidence with stubbornness. She's empowering herself! I mean, if Persephone didn't grieve about it, why should her mother grieve on her behalf? What a waste of energy.

LIDIA: Absurd. Demeter is upholding a high ethical standard.

CALLISTO: Based on what? Was she upholding a high ethical standard when she starved everyone for her six months of mourning?

LIDIA: Her child was kidnapped! What would you have done?

CALLISTO: I don't know, but I wouldn't have done what Demeter did.

LIDIA: Go on, Charleen. Ignore this pseudo-masochist. Tell us what happens.

CHARLEEN: Demeter, Zeus, Persephone, and Hades gathered in a circle at the end of the earth to discuss Persephone's future. After a quiet negotiation between the parties, a contract was written and signed. Demeter and Hades agreed to share Persephone. She would spend half the year at a summerhouse with her mother. The other half she would spend with Hades. When Persephone was with Hades, nothing grew or bloomed. These periods came to be known as the winter months. Over time, Demeter learned that she could cope with the absence of her daughter by impregnating the earth with garlic cloves. In the fall, she and Persephone cracked the bulbs in piles. They got on their knees and scooped out heaps of soil. They jabbed each clove into the earth before Persephone went back under. Sometimes when Persephone lay in the arms of her husband

and looked up, she could see the roots poking through the ceiling. Millions of them suspended above her in the dark ether like a second sky. Her mother's knuckles reaching out to her from the darkness, reminding her that if she ever chose to return home, her mother would thrust her hands through the earth and extend her fingers into spiral staircases.

AQUARIUM

Winter leaves a trail of withered sunflowers at my feet. In the sand, I know I will become unimportant. I have already picked up the thirty-nine sheets of glass from Sella Windows. They arrived several months after I ordered them. In the snow, the sunflowers become important for the mind's reasoning skills: death can be trampled on. I imagine moving through the sea of winter with a boat, a pair of oars, and light. I must reach my wife through the snowdrifts. Kiss her through the snowdrifts. When I touch the oars and feel the weight of the wood, it seems the color of life might return. I spent all winter in the garage building bases for the aquariums. They're about a foot tall and a foot thick. The fiberboard is not attractive. I take the blue paint stored in the garage and apply a thick coat over the fiberboards. To keep warm during the long hours in the makeshift shop, I've built a fire with wood I chopped in the forest three miles from here. I toss kindling into a portable grill with a tripod stand and a metal rack.

I continue to work my way through the snowdrifts, exiting the house and returning to the garage with the finished aquarium bases. The air enters my lungs and hurts them. Snow footprints dot the basement floor like flattened pigeons. As I remove my waterproof boots, the heat circulating the house begins to evaporate their snowy feathers. Sometimes I enter the house to unhurt my lungs. In the basement, thousands of garlic bulbs with slender necks like egrets are hung from the ceiling in fishnet bags. Six bags by six. They look like clusters of solid ghosts, white cheeks pressed to white cheeks, suspended deep in the basement's cosmos. The sagging fishnet bags, each the size of a standard tennis racket, give the basement a crispy existential weight, a kind of dark illumination. I walk by them each time I climb the stairs. I wonder if apparitions hide in garlic so they can exist in this world again through the garlic's pungent portal. Catholic and I plant these white herbal ornaments during the fall and dig them up in the spring. It would be more economical to sell them online, but Catholic insists that they are our reticent funeral orations. How can that be? When garlic has no mouth and does not speak. Here, in the basement, I measure and cut the laminated glass into long, slender panels. The glass cutter and I now know each other fairly well. When I place my body onto the glass cutter, it creates pressure. The cutter rolls smoothly away from my body, like a train on a track.

A series of slight taps on the edge of the glass makes the glass separate from itself like land from an iceberg. I work my way through thirty sheets, saving the last nine as a margin of error. As easily as time exits my skin, I begin to carry the panels upstairs. The blue adhesive tape holds the frames together before I run silicone along the edges. I end up using thirty tubes of silicone to seal the panels together, creating seven rectangular aquariums. They run along the walls of the kitchen and part of the living room. By the beginning of January, the aquariums are finished.

This time of year the sea is frigid. I drive the Toyota to the beach occasionally to test the water temperature. Each time, the water burns like fire and I turn around for home, truck full of empty barrels.

In February, Catholic and I repurchase two fish from a store called Ichthyophobia. The owner is a man without an odor who has a name that echoes: Lorenzo Mancha. He says he loves being a widower as he can husband many wifely fish. We bought Dogfish, our oriental sweetlips, and Pistachio, our scribbled angelfish, from him, but they died in their plastic bags on the way home from the supermarket. Catholic and I overpaid twenty dollars for each of them. Now we purchase copies of the fish. Lorenzo has many angelfish and sweetlips in storage, exact replicas waiting for our current ones to die. We continually return to him. We don't know how to keep fish alive for more than a week at a time.

Winter is brutal. We haven't earned our degrees in saltwater temperature regulation. We float the fish in a big bin and offer them no artificial light. We adopt a bad habit of overfeeding them, sprinkling flakes into the aquarium each time we walk by. This pollutes the water and contaminates the fish's oxygen intake. A funeral of fish floats in and out of our abode like exchanging handshakes.

And then there's the labor of the barrels.

Catholic is walking beside me on the shoreline. It's early spring again. We are walking the new Dogfish and Pistachio. We are walking Dogfish for the second time today. We take her from the red bucket in our truck and deliver her back to the sea. She slips from Catholic's hands like an eyeball from the socket. A nylon string is hooked to the silk dress we tailored for her the night before.

We have walked other fish before her: Olive, Sky, Drought. We walked those fish, and they came back to us, nylon string roped to their jaws, flesh gone, evaporated in the liquid darkness of Jupiter's womb. Vertebrae exposed. No eyeballs. No gills. We have learned that we can't return our fish to their aquatic heritage. But here we are, at it again. While I walk Pistachio and my wife walks Dogfish, I wonder: if a dog's idea of freedom is to roam on a leash, what is a fish's?

Can freedom exist for a fish? Was Dogfish's freedom incarcerated before she met Catholic and me because she had the entire sea to roam then? Or is it possible that regardless of any corporeal bondage, her ichthyological existence is merely a roaming thought, chained only to the authority of the sea's vast consciousness? Then, regardless of her state of existence—in an aquarium or in her aquatic birthright—her liberty would ultimately be chained to the psychological tissue of her homeland, the sea.

I walk behind Catholic. I study the back of her head. I can tell she is forming her sentences without me, perhaps eagerly awaiting the opportunity to not open her mouth again. When I am finished, though not bored of studying her, I turn my head side to side. Perhaps thoughts can enclose sadness, holding it in limbo before despondency dawns.

CHARLEEN

CHARLEEN: Where were you? I've been waiting for nearly half an hour.

ETHOS: I'm sorry. I thought since it was an international flight it wouldn't arrive on time.

CHARLEEN: Fine logic you have there, Ethos.

ETHOS: Mother, you're only staying a few days. Why is your luggage so heavy? Did you decide that for winter you'll be dressing in bricks?

CHARLEEN: Oh hardly, Ethos.

ETHOS: What is it, then?

CHARLEEN: Duct tape. I got you ninety-two rolls.

ETHOS: For heaven's sake! What did you do that for?

CHARLEEN: Didn't you tell me on the phone that you needed duct tape for a tailbone?

ETHOS: That was months ago. My neighbor broke his tailbone. He was just being silly; no one could fix a broken tailbone with duct tape.

CHARLEEN: I took it seriously.
ETHOS: Apparently.

I have come to see my son and daughter-in-law in the snowdrift. A week ago, there was a blizzard. Both ends of the spectrum, England and New England, are covered in snow. When I got off the airplane and laid my heels in the snow, my son must have thought I was a bird gliding through a snow globe. My son. I glance at my son. At his handsome face. Such a beautiful man my mammary glands once nourished. I breastfed him daily, spoon-fed him my nipples. And now just look at him, milky and white. Look at his handsome form. Hatless, long blue coat. The bluest I have seen in years. When he opens his arms, he would be opening the sky. And inside this sky must be a heart that whispers sadness like the sound of twirling vellum. The little ones. The ones who didn't survive. The ones who mistook the sea-foam for their mother's white Sunday dress. When beauty is halted, what must one do with one's air and one's extensive, untenanted future? He lifts my luggage into the truck bed. I stand very still and let the snow breeze through me. My translucent scarf tosses in the wind like vapor. He opens the truck door for me. I stand stiller. This airport is so small. Each step I take feels like crushing cardboard marshmallows.

ETHOS: Mother, get in. Let's get you home.
CHARLEEN: I can take my time as I please.
ETHOS: It's bitter out here.
CHARLEEN: I'm loving every moment of it. Aren't you?
ETHOS: No. This is silly.
CHARLEEN: Imagine if this were our Arctic home.
ETHOS: It's New England. And we're not polar bears suspending time in the frozen ether of snowflakes.
CHARLEEN: When you were a boy, you loved snowflakes. You were wild in the snow! What happened?
ETHOS: I grew up, apparently.
CHARLEEN: You sound exasperated.
ETHOS: I am.

CHARLEEN: I just want to experience a little. I've been trapped in a fat whale for seven delirious hours. They fed me—hmm . . . I can't recall what they fed me. It was very little and I feel dizzy. Do you think I am iron deficient?

ETHOS: Come home, and Catholic and I will feed you. You can stand on the balcony and admire the air.

CHARLEEN: No. Let's stay here a little longer. My stomach can wait. There are hardly any taxis around. At Heathrow, they would be lined up like ants in the snow. This is just wonderfully dismal.

ETHOS: Why didn't you come in the spring instead, then?

Ethos pulls the truck door shut.

CHARLEEN: The noise. I couldn't imagine visiting my son when it's noisy. The birds are the noisiest. And the humans too. Haven't you noticed? In winter they shut up.

ETHOS: They don't shut up, Mother. They leave. They go away. Even humans copy the birds. The humans even Xeroxed the birds' wingspans. So they could fly at the same speed.

CHARLEEN: We have a natural impulse, don't we, son? To the air?

ETHOS: Yes. But Catholic is making dinner. She must be anxious, and the meatloaf—

CHARLEEN: Let me speak.

ETHOS: You must be tired from giving those extended lectures at university. Wouldn't you like to give your throat a—

CHARLEEN: Ethos, let me speak!

ETHOS: Of course. Of course. Proceed.

CHARLEEN: Nothing you say or do will deter me, my son.

ETHOS: What's this ab—?

CHARLEEN: ETHOS, LET ME SPEAK!

ETHOS: Yes.

CHARLEEN: The air is filling my soul. I haven't allowed anything in for so long. My mannerism is just like that—full of grace and

wonder—and although you are my substanceless lover, my body
and my nose and every breathing organ crave you.

ETHOS: Oh, Mother, your monologue in this dismal snow is
just too—

CHARLEEN: SILENCE! ETHOS!

ETHOS: Ah—

CHARLEEN: And although no one thinks you are despicable,
I think you are monstrous. Making me demand you. You
are air, after all. Some say you are always arriving or have
been arriving . . . but I think you are perpetually there, in the
linguistic space, which may mean you have the ability to move,
but you won't. I can say that about trees too. Trees with long,
windy lungs that bifurcate the air and the sky, that separate a
palm of clouds into fingers. But I need you more than anything
else. You help me breathe and without you—without you,
where would I be but in somebody's grave. But you were there,
and I was over here languishing. You make long contours of
my body, running along the border of my skin. We have this
unspoken thing between us.

I promise I won't talk about nitrogen or carbon monoxide
if you sign a nonverbal contract saying you'll leave me alone.
You won't drag me with you everywhere. You won't ask me
to dine with your ephemeral friends. But these days I've
been thinking— perhaps I need to get to know you better.
Someone mentioned fresh air. And it intrigued me. Your
name came up on the airplane. I didn't know your last name
was air. I thought your first name was air, that you didn't
have a last name. I didn't think you were one of those people
that belong in a clan, but you are. You probably have a
family tree that I know very little about. But fresh air was
mentioned in a conversation, and it's hard for me to recall
the reason why. But fresh air. I need some fresh air, someone
told me. I nearly pulled a thigh or crotch muscle just thinking
about you as you renewed yourself in my mouth. I hold

you on my tongue a little longer. But fresh. The dictionary
describes you as recently made or obtained or recently arrived.
Which means, in context, you have not been fresh. You may
have been old or moldy or anything imaginable . . . which is
bad news for me because I am holding you rather cautiously
on my tongue. Had I known you were moldy before you
arrived to me, I wouldn't have been as ready to receive you.
And even though it does say that you are fresh air . . . out of
suspicion, I may ask you to get in the shower immediately . . .
and you would argue that you, as air, you would not need a
shower—

ETHOS: Mother—

I watch my son. From this angle, he seems to be shrinking in a limit-
less way. I touch his shoulder to dispel the uneasy feeling that has
begun to materialize in my bloodstream. His shoulder is solid.

CHARLEEN: You must be very lonely, son, standing in the middle
of an airport lane with your mother.

ETHOS: You came back.

CHARLEEN: Your rage came at me so quickly! I had to find a way
to stall your mouth.

ETHOS: What rage?

CHARLEEN: You know, the classics have saved me. They are
the most ancient form of psychotherapy. Reading them, you
feel that your soul divides less and less. You get the sense that
someone else is living the tragedy for you, like a surrogate being.
Greek tragedy will carry all your tragedies in her womb for at
least nine months of the year. You only have to experience the
pain for a short while—not longer than you need to. Literature
can carry all the wounds and cut psychological tissues and
beauties and abrasions. It's really beautiful, what the ancients
left us. A container. Filled with remedies.

ETHOS: But the air is not part of Greek myth, Mother! You were
talking to the air as if it were a person.

CHARLEEN: I felt obscenely claustrophobic in that suffocating
    aircraft. What do you expect me to do? Rely on Greek tragedy
    for freedom?

ETHOS: Can't you get in?

CHARLEEN: No. Just a little longer, son.

ETHOS: Moth—

CHARLEEN: No! I can't tell if the cold numbs my rage or makes it
    go away. But here I am again. Breathing again after what appears
    to have been a very long time. Strapped into the compacted seat,
    I heard the sirens of air from outside the aircraft luring me out
    of my seat. Their voices were singing to me in the most seductive
    crescendo. My ears rang, and I felt the suction of the aircraft
    breathing on me. I began to hallucinate that I was lying in a
    dentist's chair. Instead of the suction tube pulling liquid out of
    my mouth, it vacuumed out my brain stem.

My throat has begun to hurt and my son has stopped interrupting
me. I look at the flurry of his hair, stylized by the snowdrift. His ears
are bright crimson, naked against the bleached background. An eager
concupiscent voice floods my vision. It is ashamed I can't have sexual
intercourse with my son. Cain and Abel both had to fuck their mother.
They had to. They didn't have a choice. It must be an ancient maternal
yearning: to create something that will reenter you again, even if it's
just a temporary arrangement. Is it a priapic Zeno's paradox? It must
be difficult to know that your daughter has drifted away into death and
your son cannot choose to mate with her, in the most biblical sense.
The most important question is: did Cain and Abel fight for a particular coital position with their mother? "No, no, brother, you can't have
her this way. You see, I have trademarked it." I will never know the
economy of my son's sexuality, as I never had a second son or a daughter
to exercise this theory in the most empirically lavish way. This thought,
although it has remained invisible to me for as long as I can remember,
appears here to turn my ears as red as my son's. Fearing my disturbed
desires will be exposed to him, I turn my gaze toward the snowdrift.

Raw, milky skin floods the earth, converting yellowed grass, dirt, soiled field into virgins. They did say that as a woman grows older her sexual yearnings augment. I would pin my son here if I could.

CHARLEEN: I've delayed you long enough. Take me to your home.

CHARLEEN: Why is there a sewing machine on the balcony?

Catholic glances at me quickly before exiting the kitchen.

ETHOS: Oh. Catholic is sewing.
CHARLEEN: What's she sewing?
ETHOS: Tiny outfits. Little ones, you know.
CHARLEEN: This is very good news! Grandchildren! But she
   doesn't seem like she's with child.
ETHOS: Mother, the outfits are for the fish. The fish tank.
CHARLEEN: But they could be for children too?
ETHOS: No, Mother. Not ever again.
CHARLEEN: Oh, but she's young. Her child-rearing days are not over!
ETHOS: She had her tubes tied.

I am appalled. So my fear of our lineage ending is becoming a reality.
But there is hope for us.

CHARLEEN: There are plenty of fields you can harvest. Why do
   you even try in a barren one? Time for a new wife.

I can't sleep. I haven't been sleeping. I am a ghost. A shadow. Not even a guest in their home. I leave for England the day after tomorrow, and a restful night is all I ask. The blizzard threatens but doesn't arrive. We, Ethos and I, had tucked Catholic in so she could thaw out. We sat at the table and stared at the baked haddock I had prepared for them both. I had marinated the haddock in rosemary, anise, parsley, garlic. I had sprinkled it with salt and drizzled it with extra-virgin olive oil, a recipe passed down from my grandmother to my mother to me. Ethos didn't take one bite. He may have had a horrific awakening: perhaps this haddock had sampled Colin's lungs or Abby's spleen. He may have realized he didn't want to be part of the food chain his children were on. Eating the thing that may have eaten his children. I ate the whole thing, child-eater that I am. I am the grandmother who turns to cannibalism for closure. I chewed the haddock slowly and deliberately. Its thick, dry, white chunks fell like the sound of a timpani. So what if the fish was bloated and unwell. I took my grandchildren into me. Insulating them temporarily from the icy waters of the North. They should view my stomach and my throat as the mouth of a harbor.

A place they can call home. Built from the ground up and fifty-seven years old.

Insomnia is holding me captive. The night steals through me. Vacancy ambushes my thoughts and drags me through a hirsute landscape of umbrage and hostility and distillation. I do not understand this sort of rage. I find myself tossing and turning in bed, fighting with my pillow. Perhaps this blue room is haunted. Colin and Abby used to crawl from one end of it to the other. Lying on this portable cot, I begin to see their ghostly silhouettes crawling. It appears as if the toddler-shaped fog is trying to blend in with the darkness. Reality feels delayed. Sometimes I wish I could take a vacation from myself, or separate body from logic. I find my mind dragging my body out of bed. I walk back and forth. People fuck to dream on, or people fuck to stop dreaming. I should have asked my student—such an assiduous student he is, so tender toward his studies, toward me—to come with me to America. Why does he insist on visiting his family? Paying tribute to his deceased mother? My sexual organs are peeling back their curtains, and I feel so ready and available and fleshy. Why does God design women's sexual organs to resemble drapery? One must peel back panels and flaps to allow light inside. To increase privacy, God made the drapery. Interior decoration is overrated. If God doesn't want me to fornicate with my son, he should have designed him to look less like my husband and more like a teakettle. Even the way he moves is exactly like my husband! The distinctive swagger. The cruelty of that design. Most mothers fear being sexually attracted to their sons, but I don't fear this at all. I only fear that I may act on my infatuation. Grief happens this way, doesn't it? The mind is unable to cope, so it places the burden on the body. The body, naturally, can't hang on. I must find an outlet in ecstasy. I can't see far into the present, let alone into the future. I have mistaken a door for a manhole. My son for my rebirth. Where am I? Am I in my body? I find myself peeling back the curtain of the blue room. Then I find myself before Ethos.

He is lying on the sofa with a thick blanket on top of him. My poor son. Kicked out of bed by his wife?

CHARLEEN: Why is she treating you this way?

ETHOS: Mother?

CHARLEEN: What did you argue about?

ETHOS: Why aren't you in bed?

CHARLEEN: I couldn't sleep. Scoot over.

ETHOS: There's hardly any room. You can sleep here, and I can sleep on your cot.

CHARLEEN: Don't be silly. Scoot over.

ETHOS: It won't fit both of us.

CHARLEEN: We'll make it fit.

My son pulls himself closer to the back of the sofa as I slump down.

ETHOS: It's tight.

CHARLEEN: I used to hold you in my arms on a sofa like this one. You weren't shy then.

I begin to feel my son's warmth percolating along my shoulder and my thigh. This type of warmth reminds me of the first wave of noctilucent light that spread through my spine along the burning shores of Cádiz, where my husband and I had our honeymoon. And it seemed the strings of heat pulling on my skin would never stop plucking themselves, even after our first orgasm. He was a virgin, but he knew so much about drapery.

CHARLEEN: Your father was very virulent that evening along the shoreline. He could control what was coming. And yet you came.

ETHOS: Mother, you must be terribly lonely over there in England.

CHARLEEN: Hardly, dear.

ETHOS: Have you thought about moving back to the States?

CHARLEEN: And staying with you and your wife? You must be out of your mind.

ETHOS: You can find a cottage by the sea. We can come and visit you.

CHARLEEN: It would be like England all over again. But without
the young Oxford boys to keep my bed warm.

ETHOS: You must feel some sense of abandonment.

CHARLEEN: I drag my soul there.

ETHOS: Why did you leave?

CHARLEEN: Your wife finds my presence intolerable.

ETHOS: Surely you can't blame that entirely on her.

CHARLEEN: I wanted to abandon my life here, but I discovered I
had been abandoned first.

ETHOS: Exile. What a word.

CHARLEEN: I'm not Medea, you know. In that ancient classical
world, it was believed that expulsion was a fate worse even than
death.

ETHOS: Your station in life—has it extended itself beyond death?

CHARLEEN: I am a devastated woman without a metropolitan
center and without any calendar days. I am such a woman, my
son. Desolate. And I can't even call my own son a city.

ETHOS: Perhaps it's time for you to return to a city that hasn't
forgotten you.

CHARLEEN: Are you such a city, Ethos?

ETHOS: I don't know, Mother. But tell me this: is it better to be at
home in exile or in exile at home?

CHARLEEN: You asked me that in your letter. England doesn't
know how to answer you. I've asked her. I can't speak deeply
about what I haven't experienced. But you, my son, my
handsome city, where have you been?

Her tongue swelled on my tongue. It was more difficult than what
she had captured. The falling light? The rind of limoncello? The tall
vortex was holding my face hostage. Black high heels. Exquisitely tight
leather pants. My friends had drifted far into the bathroom. Their
faces, floating plastic coins, visible, blurry, pressed to the corridor of
the bar. In the background, the clinking of slot machines. My mouth
was busy; my lungs were busy. She was going to take me home. First

into her mouth, and much later to her condo. The Vegas light hadn't fallen and the traffic had been halted by the soundtrack of two a.m. on repeat. She drank too much, but drove me to her place anyway. "You are going to be safe. You are going to be safe," she kept on repeating. While swirling in her 4Runner. In a Vegas bathroom, she drank my gaze, and in one glance, offered me her entire wardrobe of feminine ardors: breasts, skin, thong, fingers, tongue, eyelashes. She was a perfect symmetry of East and West. Submerged beneath, I had no idea what corridor to exit through. She took my hand into hers and informed me that she used to be a circus performer, a contortionist who fit into a nine-inch box, and an elephant trainer. But now, she was just a high-paid masseuse. Her income was elaborate, like a Russian doll, one head emerging from another. And so on and so forth. My desire for her increased as she increased the pressure on my hand and on my swollen lips. She held my tongue in place for a very long time, as if my tongue were a stargazer she had to corner. The pleasure of holding still for those perfect lips was intoxicating. That pleasure. My God. At last, she released me back into the glittering disco lights and asked me what kind of poetry I wrote and if I had any memorized, and if so, if I didn't mind reciting it. And like most things in life, the sky of her mouth began to pour rain. Droplets of emotion here and there, and then I learned that she had just, in one night, gambled away ten grand, that her partner of five years was never around, and that her father had died of pancreatic cancer. She poured this information out as if it were pocket change she had to get rid of, as if it were a burden dangling in her slacks pocket. Making too much noise with each stride.

Where I came from: I had been at my mother's shop for twelve hours, working fourteen to sixteen hours a day to maintain her dry-cleaning, tailoring business. I had flown in months ago to help out. Her business had continued to suffer, and I missed being with a woman. To relieve the stress, I had told her I would try not to come home that night. My mother had helped me dress. "If you must seduce a woman, this is the way to go about it," she had informed me casually. Like one of her clients, she had dressed me in high heels and dark clothes that spoke to my curves, telling me that if I came home tonight, she might as well fold her business. It was her business to make women sexy.

My understanding of one-night stands was formed by the movies I watched: basically, bad sex and intoxication, and forgetfulness the morning after. But with her, it was heartbreaking. She had changed into a cotton dress and sprawled out on the sofa, exhibiting her exquisite thighs. She wanted to watch *La Vie en Rose* with me at 2 a.m., so we watched *La Vie en Rose* at 2 a.m. I didn't know if it was okay, under the one-night-stand rule, for us to watch sexy, devastating foreign films. I thought people just fucked and shuffled immediately into amnesia. I wasn't prepared for Édith Piaf and her sad, murmuring voice. She pet her cat, and I wondered what was her partner thinking, deserting this intoxicating island for more circus life. I saw a few scars on her arms and wrists, fading lightly, and asked about their origins. "From training elephants," she informed me. "Sometimes they got too close." She pet the forehead of the cat while she told me more about her childhood in the circus. Her mother and father had done it, and they had taught her, so she had done it. "My father died of pancreatic cancer, a horrible death," she told me. "So much pain." She sent money to her mother to help her cope, though they had their struggles. No matter what she did, she was never enough, never good enough. There was so much wind in her voice. As if we were in a three-year relationship, all packed into one night. I recall Édith's face and the flickering emotions on her face in the backdrop. Her face was dominated by black almond eyes, black eyebrows, eyes that curved upward. They looked like monarch butterflies, wings clipped by flight, by duration and wind. I felt so sad I leaned back. She spoke about her father. Then more about her bitter relationship with her mother. I felt like I had leaned back into time. Into a place where heartache would no longer exist. I told her hardly anything about me, simply that I was a writer and teacher. She was so beautiful and so melancholic. Must beauty and melancholy coexist always? I didn't have the sensual language then to communicate to her how incredible she was—her face, her curves, her thighs, her emotional confusion, the immaculate aura of her femininity, all there, available for her partner, and I was with her instead—a fable, perhaps, on a nonexistent mantel of falling light. Though I had been drawn to women emotionally, she was the first woman I was drawn to sexually. In the most provocative way possible.

Where I came from: Long before landing at McCarran Airport, I had been involved in sexual relations with two white boys, one from Florida and the other from Nebraska. I grew up in Iowa, land of bovines and white people. I was in search of closeness. The emotional perspective of the one-night stand is the paradoxical approach to emotional fulfillment. When she felt the hunger of my desire for her, or perhaps when the music from the film had become too unbearable, she walked up to me and began to unravel sensuality from my tongue. She kissed me and peeled me away, layer by layer. She removed, inch by inch, her dress, her height, her languishing melancholy. By the time she was done, she had already pinned me to the sofa. "Tell me what you want and I will please you," she repeated firmly and gently as she entered me. I remember her lifting her long finger from the curtain that hid my hierarchy of grief and pleasure and surrounding me with a silence. Much later, when my lungs were able to develop their own photographic lenses, the vapor of sorrow I felt became my own pleasure. What she had done was traffic my clitoris through enclosure by zooming in and out, making me exposed before exposure. In retrospect, I realized I had become a tripod of some sort; her fingers, the eye that pointed toward light and perception. Images of ecstasy and melancholy were deflected and distilled somewhere along my uterine wall. I heard the clicking and flickering silence. During her opening of me, perhaps she'd made room for Édith Piaf's voice to siphon itself in. Perhaps what had been displayed on the theatrical uterine wall was not a silent film of pain or pleasure, but an opera of hysterical beauty.

Our pleasure brought me into her bedroom. The bed appeared as if it were on the floor, but upon closer inspection, in the bright Vegas morning, it was on a very low platform made out of wood. The platform lifted the bed off the ground so it appeared as if it were floating like a boat. Empty water bottles were ubiquitously scattered. She fell asleep after pinning me on the bed. I stared up at the empty sky of her ceiling. I experienced an extreme degree of insomnia as the loneliness climbed the rope of my body into the first chamber of my heart. Had I known I would bloom this way—forever into the sultriness of loss— would I have allowed her to buy me the drink that brought me here? I had left things behind to emerge into this woman's form. That same night, my transsexual friend had designed an entire evening for me and her partner. All three of us had planned to spend an evening in her pink palace, but this woman had captured my tongue and held it hostage. We were to become girlfriends domesticated by pink and in pink. Instead, I went after what I had wanted for a long time: to be touched by a woman who wanted me too. (Much later in life, in Paris, the third time around to be precise, I came to know loss as betrayal and betrayal was, then, a symbol necessary for change.) Everything disappeared that night. Except maybe the kiss that made my tongue feel like a stargazer. And maybe the way she entered me with her camera-like fingers. She made my body feel like literature, a place for the endless gaze.

CHARLEEN: It's inevitable that we speak.

ETHOS: Good morning, Mother.

CHARLEEN: Good morning.

ETHOS: Did you sleep well?

CHARLEEN: Not well at all. I have . . . you know . . .

ETHOS: You're not one to hold your tongue. What is it?

CHARLEEN: My delusions . . . my dementia . . .

ETHOS: What is it, Mother?

CHARLEEN: I was groping you last night.

ETHOS: Yes, you were saying?

CHARLEEN: Carpet, you know.

ETHOS: What about carpet, Mother?

CHARLEEN: Carpet and I get along very well.

ETHOS: Yes, though there is no proof, I'm well aware that you and carpet do get along very well.

CHARLEEN: That's not what I meant to say . . . about carpet and carpet burn . . .

ETHOS: What about not carpet, Mother?

CHARLEEN: Not about carpet . . .

ETHOS: Yes, not about carpet. What are you trying to say? Just
say it.

CHARLEEN: I don't know where to begin.

ETHOS: Well, begin in the most obvious place. While you're
thinking, can I offer you a cup of tea?

CHARLEEN: Tea?

ETHOS: Yes.

CHARLEEN: Tea, yes. Of course, tea.

ETHOS: Tea it is, then.

CHARLEEN: Do you know much about Icelandic chocolate?

ETHOS: No.

CHARLEEN: On a layover to London, I got one hundred fifty
grams of it. On their packaging, they called their glazing agents
E414 and E904.

ETHOS: Really?

CHARLEEN: And they spelled *extrakt* with a *k*!

ETHOS: Unbelievable.

CHARLEEN: This life. Imagine.

ETHOS: Imagine it's something else.

CHARLEEN: My behavior toward you last night was rather
inappropriate.

ETHOS: It is okay, Mother. I know you're not interested in me
sexually. My presence generates an opening, a new kind of
birth, which can easily be mistaken for lust.

What is a lie but a procrastination of truth? Aren't we just dice
tossed on the green lawn of existence? My numbers are coming up. My
head is filled with madness again. I am sorry for what I have become.
I am sorry I haven't guided my conscience into the light. Perhaps my
son is waiting for me to incriminate myself. But my son is not capable
of pointing. He has no moral fingers. In his sorrow, he has forgotten to
blame. But he has blamed . . . has he not? Perhaps it's God who is waiting patiently for me at the door of my conscience. Will I open, and will
I then close?

CHARLEEN: I did lust after you, son. I did. It's the truth. You
   shouldn't make excuses for my bad behavior.
ETHOS: It's okay, Mother. Everything is going to be okay.

Because my son isn't willing to condemn me immediately. I must
find someone who will. His wife, perhaps. Yes, it's time for her to eat
me alive. I find her in the bedroom. The door opens into the room's
brightness. Only in light does the shadow of morality have the illumination it needs to collapse.

CATHOLIC: Perhaps you did lust for him. Perhaps you were capable
   of many things. Before me you are a mother. Before me you are
   also a woman. I have learned to distinguish between you as mother
   behaving as mother, and you as woman behaving as woman.
CHARLEEN: You have overcompensated for my existence. You have
   gone too far into another fragment of reality, another dimension
   of thought that excludes responsibility for my behavior.
CATHOLIC: Why are you so hard on yourself? Why must you
   self-incriminate? Why must you stay longer in your thoughts
   than you need to?

I have taken myself far into the future. Had I known they would
respond this way, I would not have turned to them for reprisal. They
stand before me as I become a clumsy shadow, taking my breath back
into light. Did I expect Lucifer to open his hands and embrace me? I
have known the dreamer inside me is out of control. I have fantasized
too much about my conduct, and I have stopped breathing. There is an
element of death in everything I touch. How can I convey the impos-
sibility of imprecision? The decision I made last night has become stale.
Yet this morning I had begged the hard-crusted bread to return to the
oven, to be sticky and doughy and perhaps become flour again. Why
must I turn my head back to scrutinize the flaws of my shadow? Why
can't I turn my face and gaze forward? Forward is a continual beginning,
light exchanging hands with light. There is no pain and no void in the
future. I take one step forward. The beautiful mouth, the golden hair.

The evening before I go back to England, another bout of insomnia. I walk around their house in the middle of the night. I see my son, his back against the long body of the aquarium. He is cradling something. In the dark, it is difficult to tell what he is cradling. But the moon comes and turns on her flashlight. I see the teal pair of heels digging into his stomach. I gently lift a blanket over him. And over the heels.

CALLISTO & LIDIA

INTERVIEW

Interview with Callisto and Lidia, by reporter Rafael Alberti Isabel.
A year after the tragedy.

RAFAEL: So let's start at the beginning. What happened?

LIDIA: Well, if we start at the very beginning, it would be when
Ethos met Catholic. If we start at the beginning of this tragedy
specifically, it would be the children. Crawling on the sand bed.
Unattended.

CALLISTO: The beginning was when we came into Catholic's and
Ethos's lives. But if we're starting with the tragedy, that would
be when Catholic was busy resuscitating Ethos.

RAFAEL: Yes, let's begin with the tragedy.

LIDIA: It was Catholic, the strongest swimmer of us all, who
rescued him and pulled him in. She lifted him like a boat.

CALLISTO: He hung onto her like a mermaid. He was flapping
everywhere. And it was I who lifted him like a boat! Catholic

was incapable of such a manly endeavor. She did, however, find him under the water and float him close to shore. I don't know how she did it, but she did it.

LIDIA: I get your point about the lift. But the flapping? He was unconscious by then. How could he have flapped?

CALLISTO: I was carrying him, so naturally I had the clearest view of his body. Maybe Catholic was behind me to assist him in his flapping.

LIDIA: That is absurd. Why would she flap his arms if she were busy reviving him?

CALLISTO: She hadn't started reviving him yet. I had to move him away from the water first and set him down on the sand before she could give him CPR.

LIDIA: Even with that logic, why would she flap his arms?

CALLISTO: I don't know. Maybe I was carrying him up and down, so his arms moved up and down.

LIDIA: You see, we were having a picnic on the beach. We brought our beach towels, a loaf of bread. But before you know it, the Romulus children had been washed away by the sea.

CALLISTO: Poor Catholic.

LIDIA: Abby had the chubbiest cheeks.

CALLISTO: Colin was always getting into things. We were there when they came into the world.

LIDIA: They were so adorable. It wasn't like she chose her husband over the children. She had no choice.

CALLISTO: She was responding most naturally to a drowning. Her husband was bobbing up and down like a cork on the waves.

LIDIA: Why did he go so far out?

CALLISTO: He was so far out.

RAFAEL: How far out?

LIDIA: At least fifty feet.

CALLISTO: You couldn't have seen him in the water if he was that far out.

LIDIA: At least that far. Even if he were a dot, I could still see him.

CALLISTO: Max twenty-five feet. And then when we all saw him, she dove right into the sea. She was the first to dive, and then I went after her.

LIDIA: I dove in after Callisto. The children were busy crawling around in the sand bed. It didn't occur to us that they shouldn't have been left unattended.

RAFAEL: Reports stated that the sea and the beach were desolate. Was that accurate reporting?

CALLISTO: Well, there were a few people walking their dogs. But they were far-off.

LIDIA: They left footprints. But when the water ebbed and flowed, the footprints got washed away like the children. When the accident happened, it was just us six. Ethos, Catholic, Callisto, me, and the two Romulus children.

CALLISTO: It was as if the sea had sinister motives. Like a wolf waiting for the pack to disperse so he could begin his attack.

LIDIA: Like, "I can't take your husband, but your children, I'll take them." That sort of calculating effect. The sea is always after young meat. The fleshier the better, it seems.

CALLISTO: I brought him in. Catholic did CPR on him.

LIDIA: It was an emotional, hydraulic thing for her.

CALLISTO: One moment her husband was drowning.

LIDIA: The next moment she resurrected him. Overjoyed with his rebirth.

CALLISTO: And then, after the celebration, the realization hit.

LIDIA: Where were the children? She went into a terrible panic. I would've responded the same way.

CALLISTO: Catholic asked us first, as if to blame us for their disappearance.

LIDIA: She jokingly asked if we had hid them in our picnic baskets.

CALLISTO: One in each basket.

LIDIA: She thrashed through the beach towels, lifted up both of the baskets' covers.

CALLISTO: She said, "Is this a joke? Where are the children?"

LIDIA: I mean, if someone is drowning, not everyone should dive in to help! They should have had that painted in red or blue somewhere so we could read it in dire situations. Something about watching out for the children.

CALLISTO: Catholic just went crazy. And Ethos was just coming back to life. He was busy coughing fluid out of his chest. He was so disoriented.

LIDIA: I remember Catholic repeating, "Come to, my love. Come to, my love," over and over. After that, there was the unimaginable scream.

RAFAEL: What was that unimaginable scream like?

CALLISTO: Like her uterus had been torn out of her.

LIDIA: She was so incredibly vulnerable. Exposed, like branches in a thunderstorm. And then she stopped screaming.

CALLISTO: She had—they both had—this dazed look. Like they couldn't believe it. She spent the entire day and night roaming the beach like a lost electrical voltage.

LIDIA: It wasn't like there was much to search. It wasn't like searching for little children in a house, where they might hide under the bed or in the closet or under the sheets. She couldn't have lifted up the entire sea to see what it concealed.

CALLISTO: There was the beach, and then there was the sea.

LIDIA: Not a single bush in sight. For the children to hide in.

CALLISTO: Catholic did wonder for a time whether someone had walked by and snatched them.

LIDIA: It was so unlikely. The whole thing was so brief and remote.

CALLISTO: We all wanted the possibility that they were alive.

LIDIA: We wanted it so badly.

RAFAEL: It was reported that no bodies were ever found.

CALLISTO: This is still true.

LIDIA: You hear of all these stories, of discarded bodies returning to the shore, but not the Romulus children. We never saw or heard of them washing back up.

CALLISTO: Catholic and Ethos searched up and down. It's been a year now, and they still search and search. They've searched every beach within a five hundred–mile radius.

LIDIA: The strangest thing is that no one was ever found.

RAFAEL: Who should be blamed for this tragedy?

CALLISTO: I don't know . . . parents should be responsible for their children. We took our boat out and helped them search for the children for almost a year. Catholic insisted! She was so persistent about fishing them out of the sea. But that's two out of billions of sea life. We couldn't expect Colin and Abby to float right onto the fishing rod. Or into the buckets we dipped in the sea. Or the fishnets we plunged in and out of the water.

LIDIA: Yes, we were at sea a lot. Along the river. On a boat. Catholic and Ethos were such responsible parents. They were so involved in the lives of their children. Ethos was the principal at William Blake Elementary.

CALLISTO: Blame is such a charged word. Those questions of blame or the blamable, of who to blame, or if there is anybody to blame . . . it seems . . . it seems like it's more about, what now?

LIDIA: How to move forward.

CALLISTO: What to move forward to.

LIDIA: Or backward to.

CALLISTO: There is always the backward.

LIDIA: The body bending backward for the past.

CALLISTO: It seems more like the mind, or something else.

LIDIA: It's more like the skin is peeled off and bending backward to graft itself back onto the body.

CALLISTO: What skin?

LIDIA: The emotional skin.

CALLISTO: What kind of talk is this? Have you tried peeling an apple and then taping its skin back on?

LIDIA: No. Of course not.

CALLISTO: I didn't think so.

LIDIA: But doctors do it all the time. They remove the skin from the thigh and graft it to the neck of a burn victim. It happens all the time.

RAFAEL: How did Ethos respond when he came to?

CALLISTO: He didn't have any response whatsoever.

RAFAEL: Nothing? That's hard to believe.

LIDIA: That's not how I remember it. He was holding onto Catholic, holding whatever was available to him. Her legs at first, then her stomach, and then her toes. He was pulling on her naked toes and she was crawling on the sand before he enveloped her.

CALLISTO: She was all he had left, or all they had left.

LIDIA: He was pulling on her so hard her toes cracked. Like he'd accidentally become a masseuse.

CALLISTO: You remember all of this?

LIDIA: Naturally! It's not every day a man crawls out from the sea like a baby octopus and hangs onto a few toes for dear life.

CALLISTO: The memory sounds plausible, I suppose. It's something Ethos would do.

RAFAEL: Are you to blame for the children's deaths?

LIDIA: Are you blaming us?

CALLISTO: Seems like the reporter is biased. (Sotto voce.)

RAFAEL: I was just asking . . .

LIDIA: Ethos's mother was supposed to return from an Odd Nerdrum exhibit in Boston, but she didn't make the train on time to babysit the children so we could enjoy the picnic with just us adults.

CALLISTO: She didn't show up.

LIDIA: Catholic and Ethos brought the children with them.

RAFAEL: Who's to blame, though?

CALLISTO: As I stated earlier, the responsibility for the children falls on the parents.

LIDIA: But we didn't have to dive in. We could have looked after their children.

CALLISTO: They didn't ask us to.

LIDIA: Well, how could they have? Catholic was in panic mode.

CALLISTO: Are you saying that we shouldn't have panicked with her? Because if she could panic, we could too.

LIDIA: I feel a little bit responsible for their deaths or disappearances or whatever.

CALLISTO: Oh my God! What is it with women and guilt? Their generous sense of self-incrimination!

LIDIA: Oh please, Callisto.

CALLISTO: No one is at fault! It happens! We humans get over things. We adapt. We change.

LIDIA: Maybe getting over things is a bit overrated! Maybe we should think about these things before we cut off our emotional limbs completely.

CALLISTO: So you're telling me that women are not only quick to incriminate themselves, but that they also have to drag their guilt on and on so it becomes another source of self-deprecation. *Self-deprecation.* Am I using that word the right way?

RAFAEL: I think—

LIDIA: Maybe guilt should be exploited for the depth it adds to the emotional evolution of a species. There's no better time than when you lose a child and it may or may not be your own fault.

CALLISTO: Are you saying what I think you're saying?

LIDIA: You hear about sea creatures all the time. They're constantly discovering new species. Species that have existed for fifteen million years. Just the other day or something. The people with the oxygen tanks . . . no, no, no not the old people or the smokers at the casino . . . but the scuba divers, yes, those are the words I was searching for . . . discover the

Hoff, the yeti crabs. The biologists named it that way because it had a hirsute body like David Hasselhoff. You know David Hasselhoff, right?

RAFAEL: I don't know him personally, but I know who he is. That actor who plays a lifeguard, always running around without a shirt.

LIDIA: Why throw guilt away when it's a gift?

CALLISTO: For Jesus Christ. Guilt existed even before fire.

LIDIA: Can you imagine being named Stalked Barnacles or Devil's Punchbowl? Even sea life enjoys impersonal and wicked cocktails once in a while. Maybe it's not simply guilt. Maybe it's a complex form of guilt.

CALLISTO: It's called nonsense.

LIDIA: Or a very complex primitive emotion located in the hypodermal vents.

RAFAEL: We're getting off topic. Are you familiar with the community's reaction to or involvement in the tragedy?

LIDIA: They created a bakery. The women baked pecan pie, lemon pie, peach pie, pumpkin pie, muffins, casseroles, even though Thanksgiving and Christmas had come and gone.

CALLISTO: It didn't seem like they would ever stop. They raked everything from their gardens and baked it away.

RAFAEL: Grief and baking seem to go so well together.

LIDIA: But people baked so they could eat, and if they ate, they wouldn't have to say anything about the tragedy. And they wouldn't have to respond to each other or to Catholic, who kept on asking if they had seen little Colin and Abby.

CALLISTO: Each person gained at least ten pounds from the adversity.

LIDIA: I mean, everyone got inflated! Not like in Jenny Saville's paintings, but we even saw flesh on scrawny Margaret. And anorexic Jimmy!

CALLISTO: But the Romuluses never gained a pound.

LIDIA: I think they lost half a dozen each.

CALLISTO: They must not have eaten any of it. Do you think they
repackaged the pies and sweets and sold them on eBay?

LIDIA: Surely not. They probably froze them for after the
apocalypse.

CALLISTO: I think the community should have given them U.S.
savings bonds instead of perishable pies.

LIDIA: Callisto. What would *they* have done with approximately
two hundred U.S. savings bonds? They wouldn't have gained
hardly any interest from them.

CALLISTO: It just seems like the patriotic thing to do. Invest in
our nation in times of crisis. I gave the Romuluses one hundred-
dollar U.S. savings bond. In twenty years or so, the value will
double! It's awesome. It seems like I'm giving them a lot, but it
only cost me fifty bucks.

LIDIA: Geez, why didn't I think of that?

CALLISTO: You laugh at me now. But I tell you, in twenty years,
I'll be laughing.

RAFAEL: I think that's it. That's the end of the interview. Any last
comments you wish to make?

LIDIA: I don't think so.

CALLISTO: Why don't you ask us what else we brought for the
picnic that day?

RAFAEL: Sure, what else did you, Lidia, Catholic, and Ethos
bring for the picnic the day Colin and Abby disappeared into
the sea?

CALLISTO: Let me see. We brought salami, goat cheese, sliced
tomatoes with corn and feta, bean salad, watermelon, figs,
chips, spicy sunflower seeds, guacamole, grilled peaches, and
red wine. We didn't bring any lemonade, and Abby wanted it so
bad. She kept on saying, "Lemme. Lemme."

LIDIA: I believe she said, "Let me. Let me."

CALLISTO: No. No. She said, in her baby voice, "Lemme.

Lemme." Which could only be translated to lemonade and nothing else.

LIDIA: And we forgot to bring a knife. We couldn't cut the bread or the cheese or the salami or anything. We had to pinch everything with our fingers. The salami was the most difficult thing to pinch. There was no grip. It kept on slipping, so we took turns passing it around and biting into it as if it were the Last Supper. The salami had the texture of coagulated blood.

CATHOLIC

Your face is bound by light, Ethos.

In my head, I am talking to him. I'm walking to him. Really, I am. In my head. A basket of grief floats among the trees. Beauty revolving in circles. The timeless scream of hate and renewal. I stand in the kitchen, condemning the water pipe and glaring at things condescendingly. Time and water always rub each other the wrong way. There is rupture and dissonance everywhere. I am exhausted. I am. I am so tired. Of fighting with Ethos, fighting myself, the dead children, fighting the gods. It's over and done. Come on. Move on, Catholic. Move on constantly.

There is so much of you and me that I can't keep. There is longing. So much longing. I am afraid to be so incomplete. I am afraid of dark conquests. All the light migrates from your face, Ethos, and gathers at the table. I haven't wanted to touch you. I am afraid most of all. The resistance in your stanza. So remote, like a refrain. A refrain of clicking heels; I hear them all the time. The heels in those heels. Heels and healing. Mine, not yours. And I feel so out of place, Ethos. I do. Am I talking to you? Am I talking to myself? My voice is held captive by my vocal folds. Everything, of course, is blooming. Of course, there is plenty of room for sound to form and to be absolutely round. This morning. In my office. At work, of all places, I googled São Paulo. But São Paulo isn't round. It's flat. Its flatness shapes my mood for the entire day. I am a pancake.

This morning I made a mistake. I read your letter. It was so thin and simple, lying on the table. I was standing in the kitchen making coffee. Then your letter. Your letter to Connecticut. Damn me. Damn you. I thought you were cheating on me. With a second wife. A third one, even. You hear about these things all the time. You hear about the enigmatic, mysterious second wife who enters everyone's life like a sylph. But she's real. You can touch her and indent her skin. If you poke her right. I wanted to poke her. This unreal but very real woman. So I poked it. I poked the letter. It was like poking her face. I held your letter and my frame was shaking. And I was shaking. Your letter to Connecticut. Who writes to the entire state of Connecticut?

> Dear Connecticut,
> My wife is a shadow
> that a centipede climbs over
> to find its home.
>
> *Ethos*

What's that supposed to mean? What the fuck is that supposed to mean? *Shadow* and *centipede* and *climbing*? Why can't I silence your asshole? I am such an asshole for reading your letter and thinking of plugging your asshole. I'm reviewing a pile of résumés, and all I can think about is your asshole. Why can't I plug you up?

Callisto wants to fuck in São Paulo. He wants to fuck there, you know? Fuck real good. Fuck the coffee plantation. Fuck me. Fuck the women with bare shoulders there. Fuck the bicycles too. They have lots of bicycles there. Do you know how to fuck one? I want to fuck a bicycle. I want Callisto to take the bicycle apart so I can fuck it.

Fuck the frame. Fuck the pedals. Fuck the handlebars. Fuck the front wheel. Fuck the back wheel. Fuck the sprockets. Fuck the spoke. Fuck the saddle. Fuck the seat post. Fuck the hub. Fuck the rim. Fuck the shock absorber. Fuck the front brakes. Fuck the valve. Fuck the cog-set. Fuck the head tube. Fuck the derivatives. I know they are small, the derivatives, but I will fuck them too. I'll fuck anything, large or small. And then I want you to fly over to São Paulo and put the bicycle together because Callisto knows nothing about fixing things. Nothing about bicycles. So come. I can ride it around Brazil's 7,491-kilometer coastline and inhale its brazilwood, archipelagos, plains, highlands, wildlife habitats, Rio de Janeiro, and Joaquim Maria Machado de Assis. I want to rub my weight, my debris, my dormant vices off this earth. I want you to get me a bicycle pump that will last. Don't get it at Walmart. I want to fuck it. Fuck it so that I am pumped and pump-ing and bloated and floaty, and while I am fucking that bicycle pump, I can feel the gases in my body compress. Pump and fuck. Can you get me a basket, not a plastic laundry basket, but those ones made out of sea grass, or bulrush, or cornhusk, or bamboo, or willow, or wicker, or paper rope, or eelgrass, or all of the above? So I keep the snacks in one place? A basket! Perfect. Make sure it fits. Three pounds of grapes, two bags of sunflower seeds, olives, pickles, a loaf of Lithuanian bread, a sack of dried cod or halibut, and a canteen of water. Do you think if I pumped and fucked long enough my uterus would look like a thunder-storm? At some point, I would need a grocery sack to put all the waste in. You think you can toss a grocery sack in there? Toss something in, damnit! Take my body somewhere and dump it alongside the oil spill. Take my body and tuck it somewhere. Somewhere away from the wind and the sun. I wish I could get rid of all the noise pollution in my head. Save me from me. I remember the surgery, but I don't know if the sur-gery remembers me.

The day Ethos bought *Les Fleurs du Mal* from the bookstore. The day he halfheartedly tried to stop gas from being pumped into my stomach so they could see and have more space for seeing. Bloated from tubectomy. No one could stop it. Not Ethos. Not the doorman. The surgeon pumped gas into this thirty-three-year-old flesh. He treated my belly like a balloon. Sometimes the air bubbles go into my shoulder, like a champagne glass shoulder. He inflated my belly so he could see to poke around. He could have popped it with the surgical needle.

The landscape is bleak. I pull the car into the driveway of the sea and watch the astringent horizon spread itself thin. The sea separates us, separates me from getting to know the ephemeral thing that pushes another ephemeral thing to go on. To continue with the blank hovering. The clouds take turns combing each other's manes.

I am in the living room watching Ethos construct the aquarium. He lifts the glass panes into the kitchen before bending for the tubes of silicone. I don't ask if he wants help. I watch and I linger. The backs of frames hang around the spaces of the kitchen, hallway, and living room. Light parts from shadow as the glass floats from one end of the room to the other. I watch Ethos genuflect before the sheets of glass and the tubes of silicone, watch him run the blue tape around the body of the sheets, bundling them together like dynamite. I watch the reflection of his face as it runs in and out of the glass, onto the floorboards, and onto his jeans. His face, unshaven, carries itself from light to glass to jeans to wood. Watching him leaves a trail of footprints on my thoughts. How unbearably similar he is to Abby and Colin. Abby in particular. His umber eyes dodging back and forth like hers did when she was focused on a color. Is Ethos really Abby, crawling on the floor, running silicone around glass? Has my little daughter receded into my husband? Where did she go if not into him? Hiding beneath his skin like it's newspaper. Like she used to. Tears float down from where I stand and splash on the glass. I rush away, to the bathroom.

ETHOS: Catholic?

CATHOLIC: Your silicone.

Ethos is trailing behind me, but I make it through the bathroom door and close it.

ETHOS: Darling. Are you alright?

CATHOLIC: Your silicone is drying out.

ETHOS: Please, let me in.

CATHOLIC: I can't.

ETHOS: Catholic.

CATHOLIC: Get the fuck away from the door, Ethos.

I can sense the door falling, peeling away from the weight pressed against it. It gets lighter, fading behind me. The silence the room takes folds into itself. The bathroom is dark. I can't see my own reflection. The mirror reflects the content of my memory, the texture of my infinite children as they line themselves in columns toward infinity. I am a wife who recedes and a mother who has stopped measuring days and hours. Milk transfusion has burst from nipples to lips.

I come home from work today and find myself before an empty museum of glass.

The aquarium is a serpent. It snakes around the living room and the kitchen. I walk from one end of it to the other. It's a gorgeous, empty thing that carries only light, dust, and air. In time, with enough water, it will soak up our language. It will erode Ethos's voice and my voice until our vocal cords splinter, break open into our oral past. The glass serpent will contain our history in its belly. An oral history of footsteps, sobs, running water, refrigerator hums, plate echoes, jar rattles, clicked heels, and creaking doors.

In the vacant museum of glass, the echoes of our past begin to relay themselves to my eardrums: I am pushing Colin from between my legs out into the world. My mouth is wide open. I am screaming. I feel no pain. Ethos and I exchange vows in the middle of a yellow meadow. When the wedding band slips onto my hand, it seems as if he is slipping his finger into my finger. I am pouring breath into Ethos's mouth from my lips. Light swings low and vacuums sound and space from the surface of the afternoon. Lidia's and Callisto's bodies lag through time. The sand is so clean it looks like sugar in the raw. Ethos's mother is patting Colin's head with a towel, cooling his fever. She smiles to assure me that he is okay, but I can tell he's not okay because her incisor is quite yellow. Ethos is rocking Abby back and forth in the kitchen while I stand in the hallway. Shadows from the street come in through the window and run themselves on Abby's body and Ethos's hands before they disappear back to their source. The way darkness runs through the texture of their existence keeps me wide awake for fear that shadow is an ephemeral coffin, eating light and leaving the body empty. It seems my eyes won't close for days. I am startled. The blackest painting in the shape of a suitcase comes crawling at me with its black wheels. The lid of the suitcase opens up, converting its two dimensions into three and exposing its tortoise-colored interior. Two naked infants face each other like gladiators. Their hearts have been removed from their chests and placed on their thighs. Their right ventricles are sliced, but left open to the air. They look like the curling, rubber rims of two balloons. The children grab hold of each other's hearts and begin to drink from them. They throw their heads back like old men downing straight bourbon whiskey. Ethos and Abby are tossing Cara Cara oranges against the wall to loosen the juice. I serve roasted bone marrow with parsley. Colin grabs one bone from the plate and begins to blow into the marrow. The bone burns his lips. He cries hard, like a mythological Norwegian werewolf. Colin takes a nap with his face pressed against my chest. I place James Joyce's *Ulysses* on his back. I read page 549 over and over to him. His eyes open wide when I turn *curvilinear rope* into his ear. I am five or six. The strong wind is pushing a plastic sack around my back. I feel something ephemeral is growing out of me. I try to reach out and grab it by bending my arm back. My eyes bulge out. My father is trying to slide the thermometer under my tongue. I worry he's going to make me swallow it. Ethos, Colin, and Abby are receding into the meadow. Two cowboys brand a cow. The eyes of the cows are sad. They look like black marbles rolling around in a clawfoot tub. They have nowhere to go. My wedding ring is tucked inside the elephant's prehensile trunk. The animal takes a step back. A cream envelope. At first, it looks like the letter *A* is written on it. Ants crawl on the envelope. They try to write one of the letters of the alphabet with their legs. I lower the blow dryer so the air swirls beneath Abby's dress. She laughs very hard. To get her to laugh again and again, I lower the dryer. The swing lifts me up high. My mother is screaming as I land on my head in the sand.

I stand back to swallow in these sounds, these images. These artifacts the museum is about to contain or has contained. A bouquet of light bounces off the glass. The reflection on the glass is deflowering before me: the petals of my blurred skin, my toes, my nebulous face bending forward, parts of my legs. If I shattered, it would be just once, wouldn't it? If I shattered the glass, would I stop seeing my past in sounds, in images, in faint shapes? Would my pain blow apart into a million pieces, pulverized into sand? Perhaps glass and memories are only painful as fragments or shards. Perhaps if they become diminutive and dusty like sand, they grow very tender and soft and granular and almost loveable. Then pain could slip through me and possibly out of me.

In the truck bed, I pass the polyester cord around the barrels while Ethos pulls to tighten the grip. We run the cord around the barrels four times, tugging and pulling like sailors on a boat, trying to maintain our balance. My head is heavy, filled with sand. My son. My daughter. My son. My daughter. I am afraid that if I stop repeating these four words, they will disappear. To lose my son and daughter even from my lips would be hyperbolic. The end of the world, I suppose. Or would I simply be able to go on again? I watch my husband knot the cord around a metal hook attached to the rim of the truck bed. He loops the last knot and yanks on it to tighten it further. Then he walks to the truck door, opens it, and climbs in. I follow.

Ethos drives, and I listen to the metal barrels clanking against one another like buckets climbing a well. I lift my eyes toward the road. The afternoon is bright, but not spread-eagle bright like recent days have been. Ethos pulls into the driveway of the sea. I climb out, close the door, and retrieve two buckets from the large towel in the truck bed. I carry the buckets, one in each hand, to the sea. I set one bucket down and dip the other bucket's mouth in. Water fills the bucket, and I yank it out before it gets too full. I pick the other bucket up and repeat the process. Ethos goes through the same motions several feet away from me. When the buckets are satisfied, I carry them back to the truck and pour their contents into the barrels. Then I walk the empty buckets back to sea, one for my son and the other for my daughter.

Ethos is silent. When the barrels are nearly full, he bends over a bucket and cries into it. I watch, but do not go to him. When a tear is juxtaposed with the sea, the tear becomes ashamed of itself.

Midway through, he stands up, wipes his tears with his sleeves, and walks toward me. He pours water from the bucket into a barrel and gets in the truck. We return home to pour sea into the empty aquarium.

I stand in the kitchen admiring the seams on Pistachio's dress. I lift it up in the air, pinching the top with my fingers. I study its external structure, the three different layers of translucent fishnet stocking. White spirals and sconce stenciling texture the fabric. The late afternoon light passes through. I am behaving so strangely. I know this. I know I can't turn a dress or a fish into a little girl, but my heart itches. And I think of my little Abby. Did she mistake the sea for a vast dress? A dress she could put on over and over again? Perhaps that vast dress was seduced by Abby and not the other way around. After all, she was in the habit of putting everything in her mouth. And then there was Colin. Colin, who I struggled the most with. I couldn't ever get him to burp. Ethos was always able to provoke an eructation from him, gently placing a palm on his back. I lay Pistachio's dress on the table when I notice Ethos walking along the aquarium's edge. Pistachio and Dogfish are not walking or swimming. They float in the aquarium, faces expressionless.

ETHOS: Catholic.
CATHOLIC: Yes.

ETHOS: I love you.

CATHOLIC: I can't summon my feelings in that way anymore.

ETHOS: You've been treating me very coldly.

CATHOLIC: I won't deny that.

ETHOS: Have you stopped loving me?

CATHOLIC: No.

ETHOS: Yes . . .

CATHOLIC: I just don't feel anything. Anymore.

ETHOS: Will you walk the fish with me?

CATHOLIC: I can't.

ETHOS: Why can't you?

CATHOLIC: Perhaps you haven't noticed. They're dead already, Ethos.

ETHOS: I walk them regardless.

CATHOLIC: We don't know how to regulate the temperature.

ETHOS: The aquarium is going through menopause. It's impossible to predict its climate.

CATHOLIC: Have you spoken to Lorenzo about this?

ETHOS: He said regulating water is difficult. It comes with experience. He said he would be happy to give us new fish.

CATHOLIC: Oh, I see.

ETHOS: We should keep at it. We'll get better.

CATHOLIC: If I weren't allergic to fur, maybe things would be different. A dog could have been more vigilant. Kept the children safe from water.

ETHOS: I doubt that.

CATHOLIC: Dogs are fond of children. They protect them.

ETHOS: Will you walk the fish with me?

CATHOLIC: No.

ETHOS: Why not?

CATHOLIC: Because walking Pistachio and Dogfish is not walking. It's standing still. I might as well stand still here.

ETHOS: I love you, Catholic. I love you so much. I can bear this burden for the both of us.

CATHOLIC: I know you can. I know you have.

ETHOS: Will you let me hold you?

I walk up to him. He lets go of the strings tied to the fish. And into his arms, I appear. I used to appear regularly before this door that holds up my spine. My body. My contour. This time I feel shy before it. I lean forward. My head bows into his slender and muscular jugular cave as he wraps his arms around my waist. My husband holds me, and I feel like I have acquired a new wardrobe. Each caress, each embrace, each kiss conforms to my form, breathing into me like a shadow breathes into a tree.

CATHOLIC: Will you get new fish from Lorenzo?

ETHOS: Yes.

CATHOLIC: And will you get a sitter for them? I would like for us
   to return to the sea.

The sea is Ethos's cemetery. It's mine too. This burial ground will eat anything you feed it, even flowers. I toss in a bouquet of morning glories, daisies, hyacinths, and roses. Gone. It eats them all. Pulverizing them under heavy blankets of breath. Today I carry the dead fish in a bucket. They sit in their bucket while I drive. When I pull into the driveway of the sea, the pungent smell of their rotting flesh sends me out the door. I grab the bucket and walk quickly to the edge and pour them in. The clouds are professional bystanders, hovering, watching, then moving along like a nebulous crowd. They won't get involved in my grief.

ETHOS: How long will this take us again?
CATHOLIC: A very long time.

Ethos and I hover over the bathtub. Pistachio and Dogfish are wiggling. Ethos tries to put the garment on Pistachio, but as he dips his hand into the water, Pistachio flinches. His response to Ethos's touch is like an electrical outage. I dip my fingers in. I try to press Dogfish to the side of the tub so I can get a good grip. Her flesh is slippery. I wonder if we'll ever get these dresses on the fish.

ETHOS: We can't do this anymore. Our fingers are pruney.
CATHOLIC: They're so frightened. Wiggling away from us before we even touch them.
ETHOS: I don't think they like the constriction of the dresses very much.
CATHOLIC: Of course they do!
ETHOS: Then why do they keep on swimming away from us?
CATHOLIC: They're fish. Their natural impulse is to slip away.

ETHOS: We can't just spend an entire day trying to dress them. We've been at this for four hours. It's almost dinnertime.

CATHOLIC: We have to keep trying.

ETHOS: Can't we just put them in a net and drag the net through the water?

CATHOLIC: No. They want to dress up and look nice, Ethos. And the dresses double as collars. Without them, we couldn't guide the fish around in the tank.

ETHOS: But what's the difference, Catholic. Come on.

CATHOLIC: Since they're struggling so much, perhaps we should crush sleeping pills in the tank.

ETHOS: Oh no, Catholic, I don't think drugging them is a good idea at all. What if they don't wake up?

CATHOLIC: Then they won't have to struggle so much.

ETHOS: They'll rot in the aquarium.

CATHOLIC: We've gone through so many fish. It doesn't matter.

ETHOS: I feel responsible. I don't want to impose or pressure the fish anymore.

CATHOLIC: Oh really?

ETHOS: I'm sure there's a way to make their bodies less lubricated.

CATHOLIC: How?

ETHOS: I don't know.

CATHOLIC: I have an idea. Go to the kitchen cabinet and get a plastic sack.

Ethos disappears into the kitchen. He returns with a grocery bag.

CATHOLIC: Give it to me.

I dip the sack into the water. Water floods in. I push Pistachio into it, then knot the opening. Water spills out in small bursts.

CATHOLIC: Get me a pair of scissors, a needle, and thread from the balcony.

ETHOS: Is black okay?

CATHOLIC: Black is fine.

Ethos exits. Pistachio struggles in the sack, and water erupts from it. He's less slippery; I have more control over his movement. Ethos returns, holding a needle, thread, and scissors.

CATHOLIC: Thread it for me.

Inside the sack, there's a thin coat of water around Pistachio. He's struggling harder because there's less water. He rolls and thrashes. I let some air out of the sack and knot it. Ethos holds the needle. The thread looks like a black flag drifting out of the needle's eye.

CATHOLIC: Give it to me.

He hands me the needle. I begin to stitch the top part of the dress together. I place the fish, still in the sack, on the tile. I put the dress around the sack. Pistachio struggles, but I tame him by adding pressure. I return the dressed-up sack to the tub.

CATHOLIC: Scissors, Ethos.

I cut one end of the sack and hand the scissors back to Ethos. Water spills out into the tub. I slip the sack off Pistachio and pinch the unstitched end of the dress.

CATHOLIC: The needle, Ethos.

With Pistachio in the tub, I stitch the hem of the dress together until its mouth is sealed.

CATHOLIC: Scissors, Ethos.

I cut the thread off the dress.

CATHOLIC: Dogfish's turn. Get me another bag.

It's odd, in the middle of winter, a beautiful spring. The air is crisp and clean. I'm wearing a thin trench coat, and my legs have overdosed on bliss. I walk away from the workforce, digging inside my purse for keys. A voice from behind startles me.

CALLISTO: Catholic!
CATHOLIC: What are you doing here, Callisto?
CALLISTO: I got you something.

He hands me a floral print bag.

CATHOLIC: No. No. Really, Callisto. Return it.
CALLISTO: Open it.
CATHOLIC: No.
CALLISTO: Come on. You can't reject a gift like this.
CATHOLIC: Please don't coerce me into accepting a gift that I don't need or want.
CALLISTO: If you haven't seen it, how do you know you don't want it?

CATHOLIC: Fuck off, Callisto.

CALLISTO: Hey, what's up with the drop-dead-gorgeous-woman-in-high-heels tone? I got you a bag full of pantyhose! I'm always ripping them to shreds when we fuck . . . I thought you would appreciate new ones. For work.

CATHOLIC: I said fuck off. I don't need your pantyhosing pity gesticulation.

CALLISTO: Gesticu what?

CATHOLIC: Go home.

CALLISTO: Hey, I keep calling you. How come you don't answer my phone calls anymore?

CATHOLIC: We're done.

CALLISTO: Oh no. Not that. I know there hasn't been much interaction in the two days—

CATHOLIC: Two days?

CALLISTO: Oh, okay. The last three or four or five or, fuck, six months, because of my tailbone. But it miraculously healed!

The keys fall into my fingers when I dig inside my purse again. I push a black button and the car unlocks.

CATHOLIC: I'm still on the company's property. Could we go somewhere else to talk?

CALLISTO: Sure. Sure. Of course.

CATHOLIC: Get in.

We climb in and I reverse out of the parking lot. The car crawls away from the company's vast lawn and onto the freeway. I glance at Callisto. The floral bag sits on his lap. He looks like a Japanese girl in middle school who has been banned from shoe shopping.

CALLISTO: Beautiful day, isn't it?

CATHOLIC: Extraordinary.

CALLISTO: Speaking of beautiful days, when are we going to Brazil?

CATHOLIC: We're not going to Brazil.

CALLISTO: You were thrilled about it a few months ago.

CATHOLIC: No.

CALLISTO: No what? Don't you miss our time together?

CATHOLIC: No.

CALLISTO: You were incredible.

CATHOLIC: Return to your Lidia.

CALLISTO: Lidia knows everything. I told her we fucked. A lot.

CATHOLIC: Why?

CALLISTO: Just to push her buttons. I love catfights. I was expecting her to claw your eyes out. You know how women are, especially when they're fighting over a man. I get high on that stuff. Just the idea of being shared in that way—

CATHOLIC: You're a fool.

CALLISTO: I'm telling you this—

CATHOLIC: To warn me? To put on a mask? So when she throws acid at me, I'll have taken preventive measures? What's wrong with you?

CALLISTO: Hey now. Her response was shocking. I mean, she defended you. The idiot bitch defended you.

CATHOLIC: What did she say?

CALLISTO: She said you need support right now. These were her exact words. She said you need all the support you can get. I mean, how does my dick inside you translate to support?

CATHOLIC: She turned her Jesus cheek.

CALLISTO: Like a good Samaritan. How could she have done that?

CATHOLIC: An act of saintly refuge. Psychological refuge.

CALLISTO: What?

CATHOLIC: Get the fuck out of the car.

CALLISTO: No. No way. Come on, Catholic! Be gentle, will you?

CATHOLIC: Out.

CALLISTO: Okay. Okay. I'll get out.

CATHOLIC: And, Callisto, get your dick out of your face. It's blocking your view of the world.

I am in the bathroom massaging my forehead with face cream when the doorbell rings. I walk to the curtain and push it back with my cream-coated fingers. I see the superintendent of Native County standing on the front step. He smiles at me. I think about deserting him to see how long he'll stand there for, but I open the door instead. The screen pops open toward his belly.

SUPERINTENDENT: This will only take a—
CATHOLIC: He's not here.
SUPERINTENDENT: How can I get ahold of him? William Blake
    Elementary School needs his kind of leadership—
CATHOLIC: Our children are gone, Mr. Becker. You have been
    harassing us all winter. My husband can't bear to see children
    anymore.
SUPERINTENDENT: Couldn't you at least try to convince him?
    In just five years, he made William Blake the number one
    elementary school in the nation. We were number two hundred
    thirty-four. And now, without him, we've slipped back to fifty-
    seven. If he doesn't come back, it will just get worse.

CATHOLIC: I'm sorry. That's your problem now. Please don't come
   back here again.
SUPERINTENDENT: Mrs. Romulus, just ask him again. That's all
   I ask. Please. Please. The school is in a dreadful state.

I close the door on him. Pleading is an interesting behavior. It would
have worked so much better if he had gotten down on one knee like
Mother Superior.

WANTED
Pet walker
$15/hr.
863-3260

From the driveway, I gaze into the windows of the house. There is nothing to see except the shadow that light casts. Light shines through the kitchen. I can see the balcony. Surgery is wonderful. When gas enters my body, I no longer feel. The empty-cradle syndrome. They tied my tubes. When the gas expanded, my body was not empty handed anymore. In the bloated state, I sensed something occupying my body, even if it was just empty air. Air is better than nothing. I unlock the door and enter. Ethos is standing at the kitchen table reading the newspaper. His head is bent, his neck exposed like a peacock's. There is fragility in the way he shifts his body as I enter. I startle him, and he gazes at me like a deer. His vulnerability widens. He is more naked than he was the day he proposed to me under the cypress tree. I see him for the first time in one year, seven months, six weeks, four days, nine hours, seven minutes, and four seconds.

> CATHOLIC: Remember the first time we met, Ethos?
> ETHOS: I remember . . .
> CATHOLIC: I walked toward you.

ETHOS: No, my heart—

CATHOLIC: Come here, Ethos.

ETHOS: I am here.

CATHOLIC: Your heart rolled toward me like a grenade—

ETHOS: It was the other way around.

CATHOLIC: When we first met, that is—?

ETHOS: Even as our lives combined. Our hearts swimming toward the milieu of the night.

CATHOLIC: Must you stand there and bifurcate me with your words?

Ethos walks to me, his wife, and wraps his body around her (I do not recognize myself), and he whispers in her ear, my ear.

ETHOS: Ever since . . . ever since I've been tiptoeing around your minefield of a heart, I've been constantly terrified of when and where that grenade will go off on my body.

CATHOLIC: No, that can't be true—

ETHOS: Perhaps it already has.

CATHOLIC: Perhaps.

ETHOS: Shard, flesh—

CATHOLIC: The superintendent has called me four times now. He always comes on when you're not here! He wants you to go back to work. He's begging you to. He said he would be dropping by. The next school year is coming up soon, he says—

ETHOS: It's not for another five months!

CATHOLIC: Please have some sympathy. They don't usually hire a principal the day before the new session starts. They plan these things ahead of time.

ETHOS: I abandoned it for a reason, Catholic.

CATHOLIC: The company is hiring too. Wouldn't you like to return to work?

ETHOS: We have plenty in our savings! I can't do anything else. I won't be able to bear it.

CATHOLIC: You must. Why did you get your doctorate if you won't work? You can't avoid him anymore, Ethos.

ETHOS: I've abandoned it! I'm in exile!

I push Ethos out of my arms. He wobbles backward, nearly losing his footing.

CATHOLIC: Why did you abandon it? WHY, ETHOS?

ETHOS: The children! Our children, for God's sake!

CATHOLIC: What children? Where are the children? WHERE ARE THEY? ETHOS?

ETHOS: I don't know!

CATHOLIC: PLEASE! DO NOT EVER MENTION THE CHILDREN TO ME AGAIN!

I walk away; my body trembles. He won't face the children. He expects me to embrace the life we are not leading.

I part the curtain with my index and middle fingers. There is a boy, three coffee tables tall. He stands against the screen, nose pressed to the door. His mouth twists like a fish. I open the door. Tears fill my eyes.

I stare at the boy. The boy, Helio, stares back.

HELIO: My mother said I could be here. (*His little voice cracks.*)
CATHOLIC: Yes.

The boy clears his throat.

HELIO: My mother said I could be here. She talked to you. The ad said I could come here to walk your pet.
CATHOLIC: Please come in.
HELIO: I'm Helio.
CATHOLIC: Hi, Helio. My name is Catholic.
HELIO: You said you would pay fifteen dollars an hour.
CATHOLIC: That's right. You rang the doorbell at exactly 2:59 p.m.
HELIO: Yeah, three. So, where's your dog?
CATHOLIC: I don't have a dog.

HELIO: Well, where's your cat?

CATHOLIC: I don't have a cat, either.

HELIO: Oh. You want me to walk your rat, then?

CATHOLIC: Two fish. Can you handle that?

HELIO: But they don't have feet!

CATHOLIC: That should make it very easy.

HELIO: I don't think so. Will I be dragging them? I don't want to drag any fish.

CATHOLIC: It's a beautiful day. I won't make you do that. Certainly not for fifteen dollars an hour.

HELIO: Okay.

CATHOLIC: What are you going to do with your fifteen dollars?

HELIO: I'm going to start a rock collection.

CATHOLIC: Rocks make excellent weapons. It's good you're thinking about defending yourself at such a young age.

HELIO: I wasn't thinking of them as weapons. I just want to be a petrologist when I grow up.

CATHOLIC: That's a big word.

HELIO: Rocks are amazing. There's so much going on in their heads. You just can't tell by looking at them. They're so quiet.

CATHOLIC: They don't have anything to say at all.

HELIO: Or they have so much to say that they don't say anything at all. When you grow up, what do you want to be?

CATHOLIC: I'm already grown up.

HELIO: I mean, when you were my age—

CATHOLIC: A mother.

HELIO: Are these your fish?

CATHOLIC: Oh, yes. Their names are Dogfish and Pistachio. They're both saltwater fish. Dogfish is not a dog, but a type of fish, an oriental sweetlips. Pistachio is an angelfish. Got it?

HELIO: Sure. Are angelfish the ones with stripes?

CATHOLIC: Some of them have stripes, but not all. You will be walking them in my house for several hours.

HELIO: Where are you going?

CATHOLIC: I'm driving to the ocean to look for my children. I'll pay you when I return.

I walk the boy closer to the elongated aquarium. Dogfish and Pistachio are busy making bubbles that ascend the watery sky.

CATHOLIC: They need to be walked from the kitchen to the living room and back. In continuous circles. You don't need to feed them. I fed them an hour ago. They should be fine.

I grab hold of the strings attached to their homemade outfits and hand them to the boy. The boy hangs onto them with his tiny cherubic fingers.

CATHOLIC: The fish are very fragile. Let them guide you. Don't drag them to complete your circle. They'll get there eventually. I sewed these dresses to protect their heads from being yanked off. Even though Pistachio is a boy, it was impossible to sew him pants that didn't look silly. Don't let the appearance of the dress trick you into thinking he's a girl. Under no circumstances should you encourage their nudity. Do not undress them. Is that understood?

HELIO: I swear I won't take their clothes off.

CATHOLIC: Nor will you impose your own garments on them. I have specifically designed these dresses to accommodate their gills. The gills of the fish are their lungs. Do not stuff the fish into your socks. If you stuff them into your socks, they will float up on top of the aquarium like pancakes. I had three blueberry pancakes for breakfast this morning, and I do not want any fish pancakes. Is that understood?

HELIO: Yes.

CATHOLIC: Do you have any questions for me, Helio?

HELIO: No.

I snatch the coat from the chair in the kitchen. On my way out, something occurs to me.

CATHOLIC: Helio?

HELIO: Yes?

CATHOLIC: If Pistachio and Dogfish die and you haven't stuffed them into your socks, you can sit on the kitchen chair and wait for me.

The drive toward the sea is shaky in the Toyota. Empty barrels slide back and forth in the truck bed. They rattle my brain into motion. They won't break open, I tell myself. I watch Ethos as he drives. His angular face is softened and cut by the light that moves in and out of the truck. I try to recall the last time I loved that face. I cannot. I cannot recall his face when I turn my body away from him and stare into the landscape. Desolate and forgotten. Snow dots my heart. God is fucking with my oblivion. If he wants forgiveness, he shouldn't have given us memory. I look at Ethos's body as if he were Adam. I look at the cypress trees before me, comparing the two. The tree's curved bones furcate like the respiratory system. I look at Ethos, and I look at the landscape. Did God really remove one rib from him to create me? I can't be Eve, who conceived Cain and Abel. Has my husband's breath been skipping one step on the stairs? One rib removed makes swallowing difficult and breathing nearly impossible.

CATHOLIC: Do you think if an old man takes something from a young person, the thief should have the decency to return it, or at least replace it with something else?

ETHOS: I don't know how to answer that. Why, did a coworker steal something of yours from the fridge? Your pineapple yogurt? But a thief—

CATHOLIC: When God took Adam's rib to create Eve, what did he replace it with? And why did God drug Adam into a stupor like it was some kind of date rape challenge and then steal his rib?

ETHOS: Well, he sort of replaced it.

CATHOLIC: But how, Ethos?

ETHOS: The replacement came in the form of Eve.

CATHOLIC: Well, shouldn't he have at least asked Adam if that was okay?

ETHOS: A thief usually doesn't ask for permission to—

CATHOLIC: But there's a law of volition that governs the universe, right?

ETHOS: Of course there is . . . but that's just one of many ontological views. Did someone steal something from you at work? Those champagne glasses were antiques.

CATHOLIC: No. No. The glasses are still there.

ETHOS: Thank goodness.

CATHOLIC: Why did God steal the children from us? Why didn't he ask us if it was okay before he shoplifted them?

ETHOS: If he had asked, would you have just handed them over?

CATHOLIC: If he asked, yes, of course.

ETHOS: Catholic!

CATHOLIC: I would rather have done it willingly than kicking and screaming.

ETHOS: I thought we were not to discuss the children ever again.

Silently, I glare at him.

ETHOS: If he took Adam's rib to create Eve, then he probably needed Colin and Abby to expand the universe. He probably used them to make new stars.

CATHOLIC: Aren't there enough stars already?

ETHOS: A few more can't hurt.

Ethos, in measuring a moment, removes his right hand from the wheel to caress my arm. I jerk away with alacrity. His haversack slips down his arm when I jerk away.

CATHOLIC: Please don't touch me anymore.

Ethos turns his gaze back to the road. My peripheral vision tells me that I have hurt him again. Logically, an irreversible sting cannot be compensated for with tenderness. There's a lump in his throat. A noticeable one. I can't convince myself that it's just his Adam's apple or Adam in the middle of eating an apple. I want to reach out to him, perhaps even apologize for my curtness. But I do not move. I can sense without looking that he has taken reality off the pedal. His face freezes in space and his gaze freezes in a surreal state as he drives. He does not look my way as he tries to prevent the lump from turning into lacrymal beauty marks. Memory turns back on itself, cutting a hole through the fabric of my conscience.

Ethos pulls into the driveway of the sea. Before he is able to stop me, I push the truck's door open and dash toward the sea. Ethos trails behind me. Though I am a stronger swimmer, he is a speedier runner. In a flash, he grabs hold of my arm. I am breathing heavily, staring at him.

ETHOS: Catholic! You can't go in there.
CATHOLIC: Let go of me!

He releases my arm as if burnt.

ETHOS: The water is freezing!
CATHOLIC: I have to keep looking for Abby and Colin.
ETHOS: We can't go on like this, Catholic!
CATHOLIC: You can give up, but I'm not going to!
ETHOS: I'm not giving up on anything! We've been at this for
    nearly two years! Don't you think that proves something?
CATHOLIC: It doesn't prove anything. My arms are still empty!
    Where are they, Ethos? Don't you love them?
ETHOS: Of course I do.

He lets his gaze fall to the sea.

ETHOS: I don't know. You can't yank the sea up like a bedsheet.
CATHOLIC: Watch me.

I run. The sand is like lead. It weighs my legs down. Each stride is difficult.

ETHOS: Catholic!

He has my arm again.

CATHOLIC: Let go of me, Ethos!
ETHOS: Catholic! This is absolutely insane.
CATHOLIC: What's insane? Not having the children or losing the children? Which one is it?
ETHOS: Everything, Catho! I thought we came here for more salt water.
CATHOLIC: The fish tank won't hold, Ethos! Do you understand?
ETHOS: Then why are we here?
CATHOLIC: We're sifting through every cubic foot of seawater to find them. One bucket at a time. Just one bucket at a time, and in no time, we'll empty the sea. And at the bottom of the sea we'll find Colin and Abby curled up next to each other like banana slugs. Isn't that what we're doing, Ethos? Walking the fish back and forth so that maybe, in a moment of surprise, the children's faces will float up?
ETHOS: Come on, now. We'll walk—
CATHOLIC: Don't you want your cowbell to ring anymore, Ethos?
ETHOS: Of course I want my cowbell to ring, Catholic. *Cowbell?*
CATHOLIC: I slept like a cowbell last night. Nothing is ringing like it used to. And I'm terrified out of my wits! Do you know how terrifying it is? Things are disappearing. But I'm not going to forget.
ETHOS: What's disappearing?

CATHOLIC: The children, Ethos! The children!

ETHOS: But they already disappeared! Dead. Gone. Catholic!

CATHOLIC: We can't be sure of that. But they're disappearing from my memory, Ethos. I can't locate their faces. Ethos, I keep on trying to rub them out of my face. I keep on rubbing and rubbing, exfoliating, but the only thing that comes off is dead skin! What kind of face cream is that?

ETHOS: I don't know. I don't have any answers. Come on, Catholic. Let's go home.

CATHOLIC: We've got no home, Ethos.

ETHOS: Of course we do.

CATHOLIC: There's nothing there for us. No diapers to change. No baths to give. No temperatures to take. No "Mary Had a Little Lamb." No lullaby to rock back and forth to. Just cowbell, Ethos. A cowbell that doesn't ring. I've been so afraid to come home after work. All those memories lying around like untidy socks and underwear.

ETHOS: I'm there all the time.

CATHOLIC: Well, what's the matter with you?

ETHOS: Please, Catholic. Let's get away from here.

CATHOLIC: I can't, Ethos. You go home. I'll wait for them out here.

ETHOS: There's nothing for us here. I've been looking for two winters. One spring. Two summers. Two falls. We're running out of possibilities. We can't continue to generate dead ends.

CATHOLIC: There are infinite dead ends! If there weren't so many, things would have gotten resolved much more quickly. It's these infinite dead ends. They're driving me mad. Can't you understand?

ETHOS: Come on, darling. Come into my arms.

CATHOLIC: NO!

ETHOS: No. Of course. You are ever and always persevering with your nos.

I lift my legs and thrash forward, kicking the cold sand into the air. Ethos comes from behind and grabs me by the arm again.

CATHOLIC: Let go of my arm, Ethos!

He lets go. I feel light and floaty.

ETHOS: The children are gone, Catholic! Gone! Don't you understand? We can't look for them anymore. We can't turn our heads each time a child crawls by and think, "Is that Abby or Colin?" We have to look ahead now.

CATHOLIC: I wish you could hear yourself. What kind of optical illusion are you in? When did you rob yourself of your human sensibility?

ETHOS: Catholic. Can't we rest now? Is it too much to ask? To inhale normally? To fold our emotions away like napkins? We haven't made love in such a long time. I miss it. I miss you. Can't we try again?

CATHOLIC: I have been trying. Where have you been?

ETHOS: I'm right here. Catholic, I'm trying too.

CATHOLIC: You can't be trying too hard if you send flowers to do all the work for you. Do you remember the last time? Do you? You couldn't get hard. You recruited a handful of daffodils—

ETHOS: Daisies.

CATHOLIC: A handful of daisies! You tricked me. I thought it was real.

ETHOS: The daisies are all natural, Catholic.

CATHOLIC: The daisies were pumping floral blood into your masculinity? Fuck your pseudo-fertility! For God's sake, Ethos, even the stems couldn't stand up straight! Did you think you could send twelve wilted, dancing princesses to fuck me?

ETHOS: I felt so tenderly toward you. You can be so cruel—

CATHOLIC: This is true. But cruelty fits me. What kind of mother am I? To have abandoned my own children to Mother Nature so I could go after my drowning husband. Of course someone has to punish me for the choice I made. Punish me, yes, I can understand that. But the retribution doesn't fit the crime.

ETHOS: I wasn't implying that. You know I wasn't.

CATHOLIC: I sacrificed two children. God, Ethos, it's not fair.

ETHOS: To save me, we surrendered two children. We surrendered two children for me. And I may lose my wife.

CATHOLIC: But you see, we don't have to surrender two children. We could still find them. We could keep searching. The search team said the bodies never floated up. The bodies always float up. You know that. There's still hope.

ETHOS: Catholic. Please, let's not go there.

I am closer to the sea because of our stop-and-start motion. I turn my body and thrash toward it. Once in the water, I out-travel Ethos. I splash everywhere upon entering the sea. No leash and no husband tug at my arm, and I glide through the current like a trembling leaf. The water is gelid as a glacier. I know in my heart that Ethos won't come after me. He is too afraid of drowning. I'm capitalizing on his fear to generate space. I submerge my head fully so my eyes open into binoculars. Water envelops me. It's hard to tell when I have dropped through the cold completely. When blood drops into a glass of oil, does it sink because it weighs more? The salt water stings my eyes, and I close them again. When my head enters the sea, my memory follows. Charleen said memory is a beehive. On the shore, my memory was a beehive of colonized emotions and images. When my memory enters the sea, it becomes a mythological creature. That's what Charleen would say if she found me here, embedded in the sea. "This memory of yours," Charleen would say, "is a Hydratic beehive." It's a face made up of a thousand nostrils. These thousand nostrils sanction easier breathing but also create a thousand times more suffocation. Each memory I attempt to cut off grows another thousand nostrils. We spent half a day gallery hopping with infant Colin and Abby. *Piss Christ*. A photographic piece; a Cibachrome print of a crucifix engulfed in Andres

Serrano's urine. Here, in my aquatic submersion, I am dipped in the diaphanous urine of sea creatures, squid piss and char piss and starfish piss and octopus piss, human piss as well. I remember Colin pointing to the image with his index finger: *That. That.* Am I supposed to find my children in millions and millions of gallons of aquatic piss? Would urine dissolve the children, or would it preserve them? Will I find a religion here in urine that will point me back to milk and blood? Perhaps I will find God and the children in the arms of the urethra. The urethra is so near the uterus, sharing the same river. What must Christ feel to be crucified in piss?

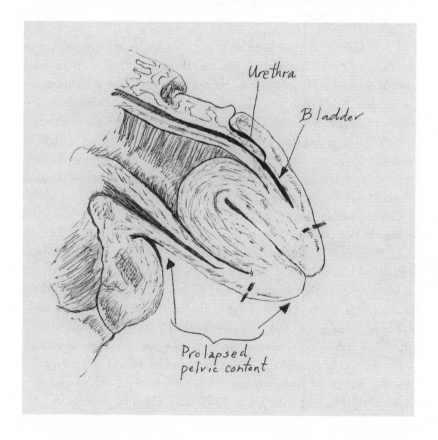

A muscular arm grabs my waist and drags me through the water. I am lifted, yanked into the air. Obscured by the location of my existence, I sense that perhaps I am in the midst of being kidnapped. The air sees a different reality, and light begins to impose its perception on me. I do not see or expect Ethos, nor do I comprehend that he is behind me. How can he be? He must not be governed by fear after all. I hardly know my husband. His hand is wrapped around my shoulder and beneath my leg. He hoists me into the crispy cold. When my husband yanks me out of the sea and into the open air, he pulls my memory from its perforated beehive. Images of the past drip on the downward slope of my skin.

I do not fight; I do not surrender. I am there in his arms, floating through air. I hear water dripping. I must be a waterfall. My husband's coat and sweater and socks are scattered all over the sand. He places me down alongside them. He tears articles of clothing off my body. He takes off my jacket and lifts my gray wool dress over me. He lowers my underwear until it slips off my shoes, then he slips the shoes off my feet. He undresses too. Naked, he climbs onto me like snow over an igloo. He rubs me with madness. I do not feel a thing, except great tenderness for his nose and forehead. They seem like the appropriate rudder and hull for the ship that guides my mind to serenity and languor.

After minutes or hours or months or years of Ethos attempting to eject hypothermia out of me and potentially out of himself, he lifts me into the truck and closes the door. My eyes follow his body like it's etiolated light before sundown. He walks to the other side, crawls in, and closes the door. He starts the Toyota and turns the temperature knob to the far right. After a few minutes, heat blasts outward, beating against my raw skin.

Naked, Ethos drives us along the coast of Exile. We pass several cars, but I do not use my hands to cover my nipples or my naked shoulders. People in the cars turn their heads backward, trying to bridge the gap between what they believe they see and what I believe their imaginations see. Disbelief is a head-turner. When they turn their heads back like that, they leave their necks so exposed and vulnerable that even a toothless daffodil could peck at it. My hair is tangled up like a bird's nest. In my trembling body, I watch Ethos while the heater tries to coat me with a fervent trajectory of air. My teeth clatter like dishes during an earthquake. I feel as if we are Adam and Eve, trying to escape post-paradise.

Perhaps we did eat the apple, but we are unable to remember eating it. What will protect us if our mental strength etiolates? God protects us with laws that govern our bodily functions, but what laws govern our minds? What laws did he invent to help us cope? To keep us from insanity? So we could bear the pain and sorrow and the endless melancholy of existence? The ten commandments—do not steal, do not murder, do not commit adultery, do not bear false witness against your neighbor, do not take the name of your God in vain, do not have other gods before me, remember Sabbath day, do not covet your neighbor's wife, do not covet your neighbor's goods, and honor your father and your mother—exist to protect us from killing God and one another, but what is there in these ten laws that protects Ethos and me from our minds, our memories, our boundaries, our insubstantial substances?

Ethos turns onto Emerald Street and the Toyota crawls into our driveway. He parks and I grip the handle to steer myself out. When my toes hit the ground, the coldness becomes unbearable. I walk inside naked and climb the stairs to the kitchen. Halfway there, I become alarmed. The boy is sitting still in the chair near the aquarium. I had forgotten about the fish sitter. His eyes lie naked before me, eyeing my nakedness.

> HELIO: I didn't stuff them into socks. I swear I didn't. They
> wouldn't move.
> CATHOLIC: Oh heavens, we can't even keep the fish alive for
> a week.

The boy starts to cry, but no tears come out of his eyes. He squints them together, either to protect himself from the impending punishment or to obscure my nudity. Ethos has climbed the stairs and is behind me.

> ETHOS: Oh, the boy.
> CATHOLIC: Turn around so our backs are to him.
> ETHOS: I don't think that's a good idea. I'll go down to the cellar
> and grab a tablecloth.
> CATHOLIC: Hurry!

I turn my body around to face the stove. My butt cheeks are toward the boy. I can't tell which is worse, the front view or the back. I hear Ethos descending the stairs.

> CATHOLIC: How old are you?
> HELIO: Eleven.
> CATHOLIC: Have you reached puberty yet?

HELIO: What's that?

CATHOLIC: It's the time in your manhood where you begin to have absolute control over your erection.

HELIO: What's an erection?

CATHOLIC: A direct point in space.

HELIO: That's not what it means.

CATHOLIC: If you know what it means, why do you ask?

HELIO: Just curious. You're shaking. You should put something on.

CATHOLIC: Yes, I'm a trembler.

HELIO: Did you find your children?

CATHOLIC: No.

HELIO: Are they young?

CATHOLIC: Very young.

HELIO: I have a brother. He's a year old. If he's inside, I can find him anytime I want. He has nowhere to go but under my armpit. But whenever we go outside, he crawls so fast. If I look away, he might crawl to the store and buy his own formula.

CATHOLIC: Is that so?

HELIO: How come all your pictures are hung backward?

CATHOLIC: They're in time-out.

HELIO: What did they do wrong?

CATHOLIC: They captured too much.

HELIO: Too much what?

CATHOLIC: Occupied space. How long have you been here?

HELIO: It's 4:13. So one hour and thirteen minutes.

CATHOLIC: Fourteen. I wish I had thought of this earlier, but please turn around.

HELIO: But I saw everything already anyway. Why does it matter?

CATHOLIC: Turn around. It's not what you see; it's how long you see it for.

The boy turns quickly around.

CATHOLIC: You'll understand better when you're old enough to devour a woman. Stay there.

I walk quickly into the bathroom, yank the towel off the handle, and wrap myself up in it. I go to the bedroom and retrieve a twenty dollar bill from the drawer. When I walk back, Ethos is wearing a yellow tablecloth, standing in the middle of the kitchen.

CATHOLIC: You can turn around, Helio. Here is the fruit of your labor. Ethos, I'll see you in the bathroom.

I walk the boy to the door.

HELIO: Catholing?

CATHOLIC: Catholic.

HELIO: Catholic. Everyone talks about you all the time. Especially the ladies on North Carolina Street.

CATHOLIC: Is that so?

HELIO: They say your heart is made of stone.

CATHOLIC: And what else do they say?

HELIO: But you shiver.

CATHOLIC: What else do they say?

HELIO: That you're very beautiful.

CATHOLIC: And?

HELIO: I think everything they say is true. Especially the part about your heart.

CATHOLIC: Well, you are certainly a candid one.

HELIO: I don't need to cut you open to know you're a geode.

CATHOLIC: A geode.

HELIO: It's my favorite rock in the world. Have you seen one cut open? It looks like scraped knees.

CATHOLIC: Raw like a cut of beef?

HELIO: Uh-huh.

CATHOLIC: You can make all sorts of rocks out of pain.

The landscape is bleak. It's Tuesday. The clouds are here mounting each other's backs. I get out of the car and walk along the sea, leaving a trail of snow footprints behind me. I look for handprints, for the silent paws of the children on the frozen ground. For four knees that sink into the sandy bed. For the liquid fingertips of the waves that took the children into a soft clasp, a distant murmur. I look for the breath of two little earthlings, the yarn that stitches them into the sea-foam, strengthening the sea's pleats. It's quiet here. So quiet. I toss in a bouquet of hyacinths.

Now that I can't give birth to anyone anymore, I feel I am truly receding.

It has been a quiet afternoon. A Saturday afternoon. Ethos and I have made plans to go to the sea, but irritable weather keeps us indoors. We are incapable of transience, my husband and I. Snow was predicted, but rain comes heavily in sheets. I watch the pluvial curtain let down her translucent laces. If it continues at this rate, it will flood, and if it floods, the memory in our basement will be destroyed. The bags of garlic will be molded and unusable. The distance between the table and the balcony is soft. If I gaze further out, the curtains of water fall into each other. Beads of water beat on the roof. Nothing to do. I open Thalia Field's *Point and Line* to unhook myself from the view.[5]

Ethos approaches me from behind. His hands are on my shoulders, lifting my hair to massage my neck. His hands wander up and down. His unexpected caress. The placement. Something in me feels

---

5. Rain and Field's words mirror each other's intellectual insights, but emotions, restrained, generate an atmosphere of enclosure. What vocabulary of time is this? This extraordinary world. Words walking sideways to the right generate reason. Words walking backward and downward or upward create confusion.

displaced. Perhaps I feel like a tree branch, ready to bifurcate if he goes any lower. He rubs back and forth, and then his touch drifts away. I hear him walk down the hallway. His footsteps are hypnotized by the drumming outside; they sway with the rhythm of sleepiness. Perhaps his footsteps are falling asleep as he walks, and the drowsiness is slowly imprinting itself on me. My wakefulness. My eyes have landed on the chapter called "A ∴ I" when his hands return to rub my clavicles, turning bones into snowbanks. He has a bottle of lotion. He pumps it into his hands, rubbing them together. In no time, my skin has been hypnotized by his hands, and when the skin is skillfully seduced, parts of the brain begin to drift into a distant place of serenity. I don't know how long I have been away, but when I wake I find his lips on my neck. Tingling. I feel overexposed. If I were a photograph, I wouldn't be able to develop into an image. The inaudible camera click of his lips. The atmosphere heightened against my chest. Fear draws me into a place of defense. I remember this place. This place of exposure and opening. Startled, I pull back.

CATHOLIC: Ethos, I don't . . .

ETHOS: You are my wife . . . I can't resist . . . is it possible?

CATHOLIC: No.

ETHOS: I have craved you immensely . . . I want to begin again, Catho.

CATHOLIC: I don't see a beginning.

ETHOS: I see so many.

CATHOLIC: You can't make me see something I don't see, even if your desire for me is as compelling as you say it is.

ETHOS: Catholic.

CATHOLIC: Ethos.

ETHOS: This agony, Catholic. Please let me in.

CATHOLIC: I can't.

ETHOS: What crime have I committed?

CATHOLIC: Your loyalty is overbearing. And seeing the children in you is too much. Everything is overbearing.

ETHOS: Overbearing?

CATHOLIC: I can't take it anymore. This impossible caress. This—

ETHOS: This what?

CATHOLIC: This absence!

ETHOS: I'm right here!

CATHOLIC: That's not what I mean.

ETHOS: What do you mean, then?

CATHOLIC: I don't know. I have no idea, Ethos.

ETHOS: Catholic, my love. Please be reasonable.

CATHOLIC: If you can't bear it, a divorce, then.

ETHOS: I don't want to, Catholic. You know that.

CATHOLIC: I know. I've always known.

ETHOS: Must it stay impossible forever?

CATHOLIC: For the time being, yes.

ETHOS: I love you so much.

CATHOLIC: Why do you speak in a language I don't understand?

ETHOS: What?

CATHOLIC: What is this love you keep on mentioning?

ETHOS: Are you mad? You must be mad!

CATHOLIC: I'm tired. The rain, Ethos. The rain.

ETHOS: So my love for you annoys you?

CATHOLIC: Clearly!

His eyes. His hurt. His exposure to the blades of emotion. It's piercing, and it's impossible to erase. I can't erase. The image stays with me as I leave him to be with the sofa. Furniture is comforting. It doesn't try to make love to me or ignite my fear. It's just there, slutless and lovely.

How can I apologize if I don't feel anything? If it doesn't hurt to make an apology, why don't I just do it? I decide I will make a point to apologize to him. But when? He has disappeared to another place in the house. The silence.

I am in the bathtub sorting through the laundry. Ethos has washed a load, and I haven't been able to find my silk blouse. I rummage through the folded clothes, tossing them in the air.

CATHOLIC: ETHOS?

ETHOS: Yes, dear?

CATHOLIC: WHAT HAVE YOU DONE WITH MY SILK BLOUSE?

ETHOS: I hung it up in the pantry! Hand-wash only. I didn't want to ruin it.

CATHOLIC: I can't find it!

Little sparks and irritations, and suddenly there is a wildfire. Ethos comes running to me with the blouse on a hanger.

ETHOS: Here it is, darling!

CATHOLIC: Why must you continue to make me so miserable?

His hurt eyes retreat, then come back to me. They come to me like black ants around the rim of a well. Inch by inch. There is no taking back, no going back. I can't retrieve the volatile motion of my mouth.

You don't think your pain is yours. But it's yours. Your mother might try to take your pain away from you. Your father might want to be a part of that too. Your father might want to collide with you or visit you or attack you wherever you are because he wants a piece of your pain. But it's yours. You must learn to hide in a box. Away from all the faces. Your brother, having eaten a piece of your pain, notices pride in your father's face. Everyone wants a part of it. That sorrow. You think it's too much. Everyone wants a piece. Everyone wants to take you away from it. And you learn to resent them for the invasion. For their insatiable appetites for your pain. You hide in the closet, and later you realize that shirts and pants and sport jackets want your pain as well. You learn that you can't trust the closet, the drawer, the coat hangers, the microwave to conceal your pain. You eventually avoid your mother, your father, your brother, and your cousins, as they try very hard to seduce the pain from you. At first their words behave like needles. You can feel them poking at you, trying to draw the pain out of your body with a syringe, and you think their behavior is unethical, and you want to go to the moral police, but moral police are boring, and they don't go out in broad daylight, and they might want a piece of your pain as well. You feel you can't trust anyone. You and pain have been friends for- ever, and forever is not enough. You want pain to coexist with you after death. You think how painful it would be if your pain were taken from you. And in this imaginative state, you feel it's absolutely too wonder- ful. After all, it's the kind of pain you like. The pain that you feel can truly exist with you. You feel this is the proper place to be. Your pain accelerates exponentially, like in a mathematical equation. You feel this is right. A right triangle, not obtuse. Right here, where your pain resides. Without your mother, your father, your brother invading it.

You begin to sense that your pain is not only desired by them, but also celebrated by others. You want to set a birthday cake out quietly for your pain. Blow all the candles out for your pain. Make a wish. You think pain is exquisite. So exquisite that when you crawl under your covers you want to lock it between your palms so it doesn't escape and so no light can get in and make you happy. You think happiness is too dangerous for your pain, so you're as possessive as possible. You don't think you and pain can be lovers. After all, requited love is just too much. Too much reciprocation will make you subdued and even banal; it will turn you into wallpaper, and there's something terribly wrong with too much reciprocation and too much wallpaper, so you try hard not to get along so well with your pain. You try to make your pain less agreeable.

But you and pain become lovers anyway. You have been fucking with pain forever, and you can't imagine getting rid of this lover. So you decide you want to be married to your pain, but certain states won't allow it. You know this isn't right. You know there are doctors who are working very hard to rid you of your lover and make you date only happiness and bliss and crappy stuff like joy, and you know there is something wrong with the doctors, and you know the doctors are crazy trying to inject you with antidepressants, and you know this is too much, and you know the doctors are being very unethical, trying to take your lover from you. You fight with everyone. Your brother and your father and your mother, telling them that they have no right. You correlate your pain with your existence. You feel that without it you couldn't live. You couldn't breathe. You would die. And you don't want to die. Most of all, you don't want to lose your lover. Your most important lover. After all, your pain is very sexy. You know you have been working hard to feed your pain, and you know your pain should be very full and satisfied by now. But your pain is one of those pains with a high metabolism. Just when you think your pain is getting fat from all the sadness you've injected, you can't seem to keep your pain fat enough. Eventually, at the right angle, your beautiful pain becomes somewhat anorexic.

You can't take any more of this scrawny lover. You know you must let go. You lie in bed with your pain, its bones sticking out and poking you, and you know you can't sleep with pain, as pain is getting so ridiculously calcium deficient. You know your pain needs to see a bone specialist. You want it to get healthier and better. You are obscenely available to care for it. But one day, you look at your anorexic lover, its bony parts sticking out, and you wonder if this reciprocal love is appropriate anymore. After all, you can't take your lover to dinner. You can't take pain out to dinner with anyone. Everyone pretends to hate pain. You know it's important that your pain interacts with other people. You know everyone wants pain a certain way. They want to talk to your pain as if it isn't a part of you. They talk to it in baby voices. They don't ignore your pain. They all acknowledge it. All of them. And you become jealous of your pain. You want people to like you more than they like your pain. And later you just want to choke or suffocate your pain, or light it on fire, but you know your pain is into that and you're just making it happier than ever. You feel so defeated and troubled.

You finally want to make your pain die, but it won't. It has a mind of its own. You want your pain to die, but you don't want happiness to replace it. Happiness wouldn't be as attentive. Sometimes it just walks away in the middle of a conversation. Happiness is a less possessive lover, just a temporary lover, oftentimes unfaithful. You don't want your lover to continually trick you into thinking it belongs to you. You love every aspect of pain. You felt you could be conjoined without having to be twins. You will miss your pain so much. You don't want to fly to Africa because you just want to spend some more time with your pain. Africa will make you so happy. Africa has giraffes with long exposed necks, and you know the giraffes will make you too happy, since animals always make you happy. You don't want happiness as a lover. It's just a temporary lover. There are knives behind that joyous face. You can't trust happiness to treat you right. Happiness sometimes walks out on you in the middle of a conversation. Happiness is rude at times. But pain. Pain is reliable. Won't walk out on you that way. Never would. You may never have a lover like this again. So you dress your pain up so it won't be recognized by anyone. You camouflage it with accessory personalities. You don't want just anybody to have a hand on your pain, to caress its inner thighs. You know that would be a violation. And you must protect your lover. You must protect your pain. You think it's all you have.

ETHOS: Catholic. There you are.

CATHOLIC: I've been very far, haven't I?

ETHOS: Very far. Won't you come back to the beginning?

CATHOLIC: To the very beginning?

ETHOS: Yes.

CATHOLIC: I don't know. I don't remember how one begins, especially if that beginning is tied to an end.

ETHOS: It's a circular world.

CATHOLIC: Pointless.

ETHOS: Hardly.

CATHOLIC: This philosophical debate. Where do you want it to go?

ETHOS: When the universe was created . . .

CATHOLIC: That far back?

ETHOS: No.

There is a softness in the pause.

CATHOLIC: I'm sorry, Ethos. I don't know why I continue to hurt you.

ETHOS: I'm sorry too.

As soon as I make the apology, I regret it. I have no right to apologize. Has it extended his sense of victimization? It gives my husband the false impression that things between us are amicable.

I have hurt him again. By mere coincidence. I glance at him quickly. He flinches without meaning to. His body has betrayed him. Of course, in this era of sloth and isolation, I am compelled to state an apology when I feel no desire to. Hurting him wasn't my intention. There are times when we meet squarely, taking equal responsibility for our feelings. This is not the case now. I do not wish to indulge in this false experience. What is expected of me and what is are not the same. Yet I often notice women apologizing for behaving the way they do. Charleen apologizes when she doesn't mean it. She finds comfort in the knowledge that making an apology will allow her to cancel out herself, perhaps reinforcing her pattern of self-destructive behavior. The "I am sorry" and "I am sorry too." The false peace offering. It's a reactionary behavior. It gives the illusion that the two peacemakers are on equal footing, when one of us is, in fact, not ready to resolve things completely. When one of us—me, Catholic, a person not yet at peace—is seduced into a moment of peacemaking. The logic behind this mindless choice: he has let down his guard; I ought to behave the same way. A false opening dressed in the garment of vulnerability and tenderness can upset the heart, can place it in the maze of the mind.

It's morning again. The alarm clock rings. I reach out from under the sheet to shut it off. Normally, Ethos is leaning against the bedpost, watching me with uncertainty. He is nowhere in the room. Part of the bedsheet has tucked itself into my robe. As I leave the bed, I feel both my forward motion and the pull of the sheet yanking me backward. Midway out of the room, I notice Ethos is standing in the hallway dressed in a gray suit and blue tie. He is brushing the lint off the sleeve of his jacket.

> CATHOLIC: What's the occasion?
> ETHOS: I'm headed to a meeting with the board of education.
> CATHOLIC: Is that so?
> ETHOS: Yes, something like that.
> CATHOLIC: You didn't tell me.
> ETHOS: Well, I didn't know if I could do it. I've been planning. This morning, for sure, I feel ready.
> CATHOLIC: Does this mean you're going back to work?
> ETHOS: I'm hoping that confronting the children will be less painful than the emotional whiplash I'm getting at home from my wife.

CATHOLIC: It would seem unnatural for me to be completely responsible for your emotional state.

ETHOS: This is to say, Catholic, if you are ready for a divorce— I won't deny you the opportunity.

A breeze of butterflies floats into the atrium of my stomach. He walks up to me, tucks a wisp of hair behind my ear, and kisses me on the cheek.

ETHOS: Have a wonderful day, love.

And then he is gone. My husband has translated himself into something else. This morning, he has startled me with his certainty. The fabric of reality tilts toward him a little. I feel disoriented. Has my husband returned to himself? What will I do? I am still in the dark, collecting the charred wood of my former self into a pile. I head into the bathroom and remove a cotton swab from a glass jar. Instead of rubbing my face with it, I transfer the cotton swab to a towel. I begin to move around the house without purpose. Trading one object for another. For a jarring moment, I am holding a spoon instead of a brush. I open drawers and doors without knowing why. I am facing the pantry instead of the shower. I stash the keys in the underwear drawer. Later, as I exit the house, I can't remember where I put them, and I have to retrace the pantomime gestures of my morning.

I drive to work, unable to recall what happened this morning. My husband is in a meeting with the board of education. That much is certain. Everything else is a shadow that hides in the corner of my head. I walk back and forth in my office, trying to retrieve it. Interview files stacked high like books. Think, Catholic. What happened? Yes, I was walking back and forth, shaking a box of fish flakes into the mouth of the aquarium. My husband said something that shook me up. He did mention divorce. Surely he wouldn't divorce me. But there was such clarity and focus in his voice. It was unmistakable. I begin to tremble a little at the possibility of losing my husband. I have threatened him with it before. Yes, I have done that frequently. But I never meant it.

The drastic change in weather, a burst of hot days embedded in the irritable winter, is strenuous on glass. On my way to work, I nearly slip on the hardwood floor in my heels. After regaining balance, I look down and notice several small streams of water roping each other translucently. My investigative eye follows the track of the water to a visible crack. The aquarium is silently breaking, its life expectancy shrinking.

CATHOLIC: ETHOS!
ETHOS: Yes, dear.
CATHOLIC: The aquarium is leaking. And I have to leave for work!
ETHOS: I'm in the bathroom. I'll take care of it later.
CATHOLIC: Use your mother's duct tape!
ETHOS: That's a good idea.

When I return home from work, the leak has been rescued by one strip of gray duct tape. I study it briefly. The lightning rod has been hidden, but there is still an electrical tension. I begin to sense from the aquarium that there will be encouragement, voltages breaking in other panels as well. This is the beginning of the beginning of the aquarium breaking down. There will be thunderstorms of glass and water.

CATHOLIC: Ethos?
ETHOS: Yes?
CATHOLIC: Help me lift the sewing machine into the blue room.
ETHOS: Coming!

I see him run from the hallway and come through the open screen door. He walks to the other end of the sewing machine and grips the table. I gaze at his eyes. The color of mildew. I shift my gaze toward the siding.

ETHOS: Aren't you still using it?
CATHOLIC: Yes, but the weather is making it rusty. Especially the needles. They lift their knees so slowly that I can stitch everything faster by hand than I can with the machine.

Quickly and gently, we guide the sewing machine. Ethos walks backward through the screen door. We walk the machine to the blue room, but the angle of entrance between the hallway and the kitchen is too tight. The aquarium extends approximately one foot out from the wall. With Ethos backing into the hallway wall, we are forced to come to a complete stop.

> ETHOS: If we tilt the machine up on one side, we might be able to make it through.
>
> CATHOLIC: Let's give it a try.

Ethos and I lift the sewing machine from its base, but my fingers don't have a good grip, and they slip off. The machine wobbles downward, and its iron leg knocks against the glass. One panel of the aquarium cracks into pieces. I lose my balance and fall backward, backward, backward, backward onto the floorboards while Ethos presses down hard on the table with both of his hands so it doesn't collapse onto me. There is the sound of deep breathing, of frozenness, of hanging in the midst before the inception. And then the air, water, and light come pouring out in a hush of a rush. As if they had been waiting for the gates to open, ready at the first gunfire of crack, split, and fracture. Waiting for the gates to open. The water bends its fluid knees and moves in a continual form of genuflection. It spreads to the border of the kitchen, brushing the wooden hem of the cabinets. Dogfish and Pistachio crash out of their broken aquatic home. Flat on their sides, they glide slowly across the floorboards, twirling lightly as the water guides them. They are ushered into an empty bay, the bay of nihil. Into a containerless space. Into the domestic space, the kitchen, where I oscillate between separation and stagnation. Crushing, taxing, wearing Ethos down to his core. Doing the same to myself. Perhaps the incarnated, perpetual lives of Dogfish and Pistachio feel the crushing, the taxing, the wearing down of their multiple lives. They glide with thoughtless surrender. They float down the kitchen floor, flapping, contorting, and flopping like the iridescent eyes of God. The eyes drift down the floorboards along the landscape of the kitchen. They descend the stairs, one eye at a time, into the abyss of the house's lower cosmos.

We follow in search of the fish and in search of our children. We press our hands against the walls of the stairs so as not to slip and fall. The water that poured into the basement looks like a dark, shallow sea. Light and tragic. I can't see the garlic bulbs, but I know they hang from the ceiling of the basement, the saggy breasts of the sky clustering our air.

We descend the lower cosmos.

We descend and we descend.

We admit we know nothing of this darkness. In the underworld of our sorrow, there is not a single boat in sight. No boater to guide us. Just our feet inside the lumpy bodies of socks as we push forward. I am leading Ethos into the dark basement. In the basement, the garlic, bundled in rows, looks like a replica of Achilles's heels. White heels. Ethos presses his hand on my back. Seeking susceptibility. We are walking back into our past. The ceiling separates us from the broken aquarium.

Ethos's hands are on my back. I am following the fish. If they wish to die, I must give them a proper burial. I am pushing through the darkness as if I am pushing fog into the room. Dogfish? Pistachio? These floral hydras of darkness, opening my body further into courage. In the dark, in the dwelling place of fear, there is resistance. If I resist now, I will turn back. Yes, there is immense darkness ahead. But to turn back would be more painful. So I proceed. I will my body forward, turning my hands and my body and shoulders back to a place of familiarity. This backward stride is a place of reparation. The night is not fluoride and thunderstorms are not made of bristles. My husband follows me and if I push too fast into the slow dark, I will lose him. His hand may drift off my body like snow does when it gets tired. But snow and fingers and most tiny things in life are not actors in a screenplay. They want to be nova stars in their quiet, small ways. They want a body to breathe into: a container for electricity. This landscape of touch and resilience and softness is a place where fear can't exist. This place of tenderness that pushes me into an immense dusk. With each step I take, the floral hydras grow more heads of darkness. My body is not a fisherman, and it does not understand the freshwater air, the coelenterate darkness, the tubular shape of awe, the tentacle rings of pain and apprehension. I must think to conquer the hydras; I must cut off the limbs of the dark. One blade to the black nebulous face that extends into my face and Ethos's face.

Perhaps darkness does not have a tangible body after all, if it's drifting from one endless realm to another. One cannot fight it as a warrior, but as a lover. Before these hydras of darkness with their millions of molecular heads, one must surrender. Surrender to the hydras. As this thought enters my mind, I feel my skin suspended in space. I drag my skin forward. The rest of my body follows, and then my husband follows. I release the tension in my body. In winter and in cold, if my shoulders are tense and my body is tense, I feel even colder. But when I release the tension and all the muscles in my body are able to relax, when I relax the muscles of my emotions . . . when I do not hold them tightly in a knot . . . I begin to feel warmer. I imagine I have been tense for two years now, and my muscles have knotted themselves so tightly that my blood and oxygen have nowhere to go. No wonder I have been dying for as long as I have. When I release, everything becomes easier and quieter. When I release and surrender, my body begins to open up. I begin to feel things I haven't felt for a long time. This elongated death is at the brink of dying. I am on the edge of rebirth. I hear the dripping of water as each strand of water curls itself into the basement. I hear the descent. I hear the lush flow, sonic and lush, like an aquatic choir. The chorus of water breaking against itself. A choral beauty, saturating and salivating.

It's true: the water is breaking, pouring in a hydraulic rush. The darkness shapes the mind; it forms to the contours of the imagination. I begin to see my children in blotches, crawling before me. An ear here. A smile there. A pair of feet. So much hope in the darkest place. How they drift through the air like seahorses. Those arching legs. Colin's face floats, suspended like a cloud, his laughing heart in his eyes. And

there is Abby, from inside the darkest residue of my imagination.
There she is! Her lips, her cherubic cheeks. There she is! I have hidden
her so long in the body of my imagination. Strands of fear and shadow
and blood vessels blocked my view of her. The voices of the water sing
in the dark. "Gloria in excelsis Deo." *Laudamus te, benedicimus te, ado-*
ramus te. Gloria! Gloria! My daughter comes crying to me, drawling
and drooling, and her lightness walks through the window of my arms.
She disappears into my body, then reappears as I press on. Baby Colin
floats to me like a school of minnows. My fingers over his body like
a halo. He glides through the surface of my imagination, a wiggling,
swimming caress. Yes, my darling is wiggling, my finger to his hazy
form. The dark has an infinite past. Colin and Abby: You were once a
part of me. Now come back into me, my son, my daughter. The great
certainty comes: My children are no longer with me. They are gone.
Lost somewhere in the cosmos. I must let go.

The salt clings to my feet. Our grief is an exiled body.

The basement is the aquarium. Of air and darkness and garlic
bulbs in bags. Are they not white shrouds of light that bear witness
to my opening? My feet are soaked, and I imagine my husband's feet
are soaked. My body is alive! Tingling everywhere. I do not know
where in the basement we are. But the sonic world of children weeping and laughing, and the tenor and crescendos and sopranos of the
water are chanting for my birth. Here in the dark, my children, my
deceased mother and father, give birth to me. They weep and cry as
they push me back into the world. Do not be afraid, they tell me. Do
not be afraid, my mother and my child. They ingeminate the same sentence over and over. My children are pushing me out of their conjoined
womb and their infantile fatherland, pushing me to the edges of their
cervices. My children are giving birth to me, legs spread. And they cry.
They cry fiercely. I hold on to the last tear, the last blood vessel, to eyelids and fingertips, to earlobes, to the rim of the kidney and spleen,
to the placenta and the scrotum, to the last strand of the umbilical
edge, and when there is nothing left to hang on to, to fight for, I break
open into the world. The silence is complete. A silence that smells like

biodegradable radiation. And then I scream hard for the first time in my life. Unrestrained. Fearless. I scream for all the wounds. I scream for all the fears. I scream because I can breathe on my own again. Yes, I must make use of my new lungs: small bands of ribs and voices. I scream. I am screaming with succulent delight. I am screaming, arching my body back and throwing the disc of voice and hurling it into the black nebulous walls of the basement. Hurling sound into air, hurling accelerated air into air. I scream and scream and scream. This liberty. This voluptuous moment. This band of light. What voice of superiority and supremacy. This place of primacy. I am here and there all at once. In broad brushstrokes, I make my first human mark on the black canvas of life. Today I am a child again. I have been a window to my ancient mother and father. Ethos gently presses his hand on my back after I stop screaming. He is there to receive me. He pulls me into his arms so my back is to his chest. My fingers are tingling. My eyes are tingling. Every edge of my body is tingling. I feel so alive and fertile. He presses his face into my hair and smells me, inhaling deeply as if I am a newborn. Then he presses his lips to my head, and he kisses me ardently and endlessly. He kisses each strand, each fiber, each curve of my head as if he is baptizing me with his breath and his saliva and his christened manhood. The way his arms secure me to his chest reminds me of roller coaster rides with my father. When the metal belt locked my body in place beside him, I felt so protected. This father, this husband, this sentry of mine. Here you are. Take me to a place without fear. In his arms I surrender every known second of my existence. He is my liquid. My molecules. He is my fiber. My other half. He is my ember. My coal. He is my cinder. My ash. He is my residue. My residuum. He is, most of all, my husband, protector of my solitude.

Ethos turns my body around so I am facing him. Although I can't see his eyes in the dark, I know that mouth. The mouth that mounts my mouth before surrendering its tongue. He holds my breath in his breath. My mouth in his mouth. He runs his hands over my body, his fingers pressing placid pools of tenderness to my spine. The softness of his caress. He gently circles the rim of my mouth, then pulls my head back to one side like a curtain. He begins to kiss, one kiss at a time, along the edge of my neck. He kisses my shoulder, and he kisses along my clavicle. Then he bends down, and in one accelerated gesture of agile virility, like a bullfighter swiftly lifting the cape from the face of the bull, he lifts me into his arms and lays me down on the shallow pool of the basement floor. The audacious coolness of the water on my skin. I lie there for what seems like an endless breath between two notes: one life and one death, exposed to this creature of the unknown. In this space of absence, in this space of exactness, in this space of sweet lingering. I hear the clinking of his belt. The crack of one metallic button snapping. His zipper. The rustling sound of his jeans.

This space of waiting.

I become convulsive before him. But my husband's thighs are muscular and they pin me down. I have become a prisoner of his body.

And when I think I can't take it anymore, when I think my husband is going to orbit the oral space of my desire forever, he thrusts in. He holds there, his tenderness tucked inside of me. He holds that space. That space of complete abandonment and surrender. The pleasure. In this private place between tenderness and sexual oblation, devotion, ardor, and deep affection form.

I begin to sense some life-form is birthing within me. I know that moment of germination. That moment of pure knowledge that something beautiful and young and benevolent is growing inside of me again. The same feeling I had long ago, when Colin and Abby signed a nine-month contract made of placenta and vascular tissue and oxygen and blood and rented out a little cottage in my body and grew.

I remember standing in the middle of the highway near the sea. I noticed something unusual. On that glistering asphalt, cracking open at the center, a delicate white morning glory was pushing out from the bituminous ground. In the middle of the road.

Coffee House Press began as a small letterpress operation in 1972 and has grown into an internationally renowned nonprofit publisher of literary fiction, essay, poetry, and other work that doesn't fit neatly into genre categories.

Coffee House is both a publisher and an arts organization. Through our *Books in Action* program and publications, we've become interdisciplinary collaborators and incubators for new work and audience experiences. Our vision for the future is one where a publisher is a catalyst and connector.

LITERATURE
is not the same thing as
PUBLISHING

FUNDER ACKNOWLEDGMENTS

Coffee House Press is an internationally renowned independent book publisher and arts nonprofit based in Minneapolis, MN; through its literary publications and *Books in Action* program, Coffee House acts as a catalyst and connector—between authors and readers, ideas and resources, creativity and community, inspiration and action.

Coffee House Press books are made possible through the generous support of grants and donations from corporations, state and federal grant programs, family foundations, and the many individuals who believe in the transformational power of literature. This activity is made possible by the voters of Minnesota through a Minnesota State Arts Board Operating Support grant, thanks to the legislative appropriation from the arts and cultural heritage fund, along with a grant from the Wells Fargo Foundation Minnesota. Coffee House also receives major operating support from the Amazon Literary Partnership, the Bush Foundation, the Jerome Foundation, The McKnight Foundation, Target, and the National Endowment for the Arts (NEA). To find out more about how NEA grants impact individuals and communities, visit www.arts.gov.

Coffee House Press receives additional support from the Elmer L. & Eleanor J. Andersen Foundation; the David & Mary Anderson Family Foundation; the Buuck Family Foundation; the Carolyn Foundation; the Dorsey & Whitney Foundation; Dorsey & Whitney LLP; the Knight Foundation; the Rehael Fund of the Minneapolis Foundation; the Matching Grant Program Fund of the Minneapolis Foundation; the Schwab Charitable Fund; Schwegman, Lundberg & Woessner, P.A.; the Scott Family Foundation; the US Bank Foundation; VSA Minnesota for the Metropolitan Regional Arts Council; the Archie D. & Bertha H. Walker Foundation; and the Woessner Freeman Family Foundation in honor of Allan Kornblum.

THE PUBLISHER'S CIRCLE OF
COFFEE HOUSE PRESS

Publisher's Circle members make significant contributions to Coffee House Press's annual giving campaign. Understanding that a strong financial base is necessary for the press to meet the challenges and opportunities that arise each year, this group plays a crucial part in the success of Coffee House's mission.

Recent Publisher's Circle members include many anonymous donors, Mr. & Mrs. Rand L. Alexander, Suzanne Allen, Patricia A. Beithon, Bill Berkson & Connie Lewallen, the E. Thomas Binger & Rebecca Rand Fund of the Minneapolis Foundation, Robert & Gail Buuck, Claire Casey, Louise Copeland, Jane Dalrymple-Hollo, Ruth Stricker Dayton, Jennifer Kwon Dobbs & Stefan Liess, Mary Ebert & Paul Stembler, Chris Fischbach & Katie Dublinski, Kaywin Feldman & Jim Lutz, Sally French, Jocelyn Hale & Glenn Miller, the Rehael Fund-Roger Hale/Nor Hall of the Minneapolis Foundation, Randy Hartten & Ron Lotz, Jeffrey Hom, Carl & Heidi Horsch, Amy L. Hubbard & Geoffrey J. Kehoe Fund, Kenneth Kahn & Susan Dicker, Stephen & Isabel Keating, Kenneth Koch Literary Estate, Jennifer Komar & Enrique Olivarez, Allan & Cinda Kornblum, Leslie Larson Maheras, Lenfestey Family Foundation, Sarah Lutman & Rob Rudolph, the Carol & Aaron Mack Charitable Fund of the Minneapolis Foundation, George & Olga Mack, Joshua Mack, Gillian McCain, Mary & Malcolm McDermid, Sjur Midness & Briar Andresen, Maureen Millea Smith & Daniel Smith, Peter Nelson & Jennifer Swenson, Marc Porter & James Hennessy, Jeffrey Scherer, Jeffrey Sugerman & Sarah Schultz, Nan G. & Stephen C. Swid, Patricia Tilton, Stu Wilson & Melissa Barker, Warren D. Woessner & Iris C. Freeman, Margaret Wurtele, Joanne Von Blon, and Wayne P. Zink.

For more information about the Publisher's Circle and other ways to support Coffee House Press books, authors, and activities, please visit www.coffeehousepress.org/support or contact us at info@coffeehousepress.org.

Vi Khi Nao was born in Long Khanh, Vietnam. Her work includes poetry, fiction, film, and cross-genre collaboration, including two novellas, *Swans in Half-Mourning* (2013) and *The Vanishing Point of Desire* (2011), and a poetry collection, *The Old Philosopher*, which was the winner of the 2014 Nightboat Poetry Prize. *Fish in Exile* is her first novel. She holds an MFA in fiction from Brown University.

Fish in Exile was designed by
Bookmobile Design & Publisher Services.
Text is set in Adobe Jenson Pro,
a typeface drawn by Robert Slimbach
and based on late-fifteenth-century types
by the printer Nicolas Jenson.